MISSY TARANTINO

Free As A Bird

First edition

ISBN: 978-1-73-366135-5

This book was professionally typeset on Reedsy.
Find out more at reedsy.com

Contents

Acknowledgement

Thank you!!

This was such a fun project to work on, and I had some great help from some awesome people.

Judy Scherpelz - Thank you so much for offering your expertise in the care and rehabilitation of raptors. Your knowledge and passion for these majestic animals are amazing.

Lory Ortiz - You are a wonderful friend and incredible person. Thank you for your insights into the family court system and foster care process.

Debbie Beach - Your enthusiasm for this project warms my heart. Thank you for giving me feedback from a counseling perspective.

Cameron Shinn - Working with you makes me feel like anything is possible. Thank you for your help, encouragement, and for giving me inspiration for the character of Mr. Roberts. Anyone who knows you will see you at work in this character.

Laura and Mary Jane - I love coming to see you at the library. You're welcoming smiles and help in tracking down resources are invaluable to me.

Mom - Your eye for detail is second to none! Thank you for proof-reading my manuscript and helping me make it the best it can be. I love you!

Rocky Mountain Raptor Program - Thank you to the amazing people at this facility for answering my questions, allowing me to wander around and take pictures, and for all you do to help the raptors in

Northern Colorado. I salute you!

Chapter 1

I t was a few minutes before the bell rang for school to start at Pine Elementary. Students were running around in the grass playing tag or throwing a football with their friends. The equipment was crawling with younger students. The swings were moving in their arcs. A constant flow of kids came down the slide. The teachers were relaxed, chatting with each other, cupping their hands around their coffee mugs.

Suddenly, a scream cut the air. For a moment, everyone froze. Students turned toward the sound. Startled teachers ran towards the jungle gym, where cries for help mixed with animal-like sounds of fury. A first-grader was sitting on the ground, holding his arm and rocking back and forth. Tears streamed down his face. He pointed up at the top of the metal structure.

The teachers followed his gesture and saw an older girl with stringy, dirty blonde hair crouching on the top bars. She was wearing a soiled green hoodie with yellow lettering on it that was at least three sizes too big for her. Her brown eyes looked wild in her small round face. Her teeth were bared. She looked a little like a scrawny bird of prey on its perch.

The bell rang and one of the teachers helped the young boy to his feet and led him towards the nurse's office. Another teacher used her cell phone to call the office. "Tell Mr. Roberts that Destiny kicked another student on the playground. He needs to get out here right now. She won't come down off the jungle gym."

Soon the playground was deserted. Mr. Roberts arrived and the teacher followed her class inside. He pushed his black-framed glasses up on his nose and squinted up at Destiny. She stared back at him, not moving a muscle. Her knuckles were white from gripping so hard.

He slowly walked around the perimeter of the jungle gym with his hands in the pockets of his grey trousers. He counted his steps, looking at the tips of his shoes, not at her. When he had completed his circuit, he stopped and glanced up at her again. He'd been here before and knew better than to rush things. He brushed one hand through his thick black hair. He stretched his arms over his head to loosen the muscles in his broad shoulders.

Judging from the crouched position and wild eyes, that she wasn't ready to come down. No amount of cajoling, threatening or talking would bring her down when she was in this frame of mind. It was best to just wait it out. Let her calm down on her own. Give her some space.

He walked another circle around the equipment. On the third trip, he noticed that she had shifted her weight and color was returning to her knuckles. Her eyes weren't as wide and her chest was not heaving like it had been. Body language was improving, but they weren't out of the woods yet. Two more trips later, Destiny slid to the ground and stood there with her hands in the big pocket across the front of her hoodie.

She wouldn't look at him, but she was calm. Mr. Roberts stopped walking and waited. Destiny was smart. She didn't need a lecture. She didn't need to hear how wrong it was to kick students. She didn't need him to ask what had happened. "He climbed my tower," she said in a gravelly voice. Mr. Roberts said nothing, just nodded. "He shouldn't have climbed my tower. I just want to be left alone." Her voice was quiet but forceful.

"Let's go inside and get you some breakfast," Mr. Roberts said. He glanced up at the sky. "Looks like it's going to be as hot as an oven today." Turning on his heel, he walked to the building. He pulled a wad of keys from his pocket and jingled them until he found the right one to open the side door.

They went to the cafeteria and gathered up some food. The trip to the office took a while. Every student they passed wanted to high five Mr. Roberts or tell him something. He made time for each one of them. When they finally made it to his office, he set her tray down and pulled a metal chair up to the corner of his desk. The cherry wood shone in the light of the green lamp sitting on the corner.

As she ate, Destiny looked around. On the desk was a triangular piece of wood that said 'Carter Roberts, Principal'. By the door, there was a large black frame with several round medals artistically displayed around a picture of Mr. Roberts when he was State Wrestling Champion in high school.

Mr. Roberts busied himself at his computer, glancing Destiny's way every few minutes. As soon as he saw that she was finished eating, he turned to face her. He leaned forward and put his forearms on his thighs.

"You are as territorial as a wolf," he began. "Do you know what that means?"

Destiny shook her head.

"You don't want other kids on the equipment that you have claimed as your own. You think of the jungle gym as yours. Well, it's not. It belongs to all the students. They are allowed to play on it, just like you. I cannot allow you to hurt other kids here."

Destiny spent a long boring day sitting at a desk in the outer office that was way too small for her, doing work that was way too easy.

FREE AS A BIRD

Chapter 2

The next day, Destiny managed to stay out of trouble through the morning recess time. When the bell rang, she pushed her way through the doors when they opened, not waiting to line up with her class, and was the first one into her classroom. Destiny's school had a lot of students who lived below the poverty line, and the school was given a government grant to provide free breakfast, as well as lunch to the students. Her teacher, Ms. Watts, had arranged the breakfast items on a rectangular table at the back of the room under a bulletin board that was made to look like an oval running track with lanes and starting blocks. The title said, "Ready, Set, Learn!"

Destiny stuffed two muffins and an apple into her pocket. Then she grabbed a juice, milk, an apple, and another muffin and walked through an obstacle course of desks to her own in the furthest corner of the room. She pushed some papers onto the floor and set the food in her hands on the grimy surface. She sat cross-legged on her chair and began eating. Papers stuck out of her desk at odd angles, torn and crumpled. Broken pencils and crayons littered the little tray in the front of the space inside.

She completely ignored the other students when Ms. Watts brought the class into the room. When she finished eating, she stuffed the wrappers into her desk. She pulled up the hood of her sweatshirt, pulling the cords tight and put her head down on the desk. Her eyes hurt and her head was throbbing.

Soon she felt a hand on her shoulder. Ms. Watts leaned close to her ear and said, "Destiny, are you OK?" It had been a rough night and she just wanted to be left alone. Now that she had food in her stomach, she was sleepy. Destiny chose to ignore the teacher and hope she would go away. Ms. Watts shook her short red hair and pressed her lips together.

"I'll come back in a few minutes to check on you," Ms. Watts murmured in her ear. She stood up and walked away. The place where Ms. Watts had touched Destiny's shoulder stayed warm for a few minutes. Destiny turned her face toward the wall and closed her eyes.

When Ms. Watts returned and again crouched next to Destiny, her hand gently rubbed Destiny's back. "Destiny. It's math time. I know you are good at math. Please come and join us." Destiny shook her head and writhed her shoulders to shake off Ms. Watts' hand. Ms. Watts persisted. Finally, Destiny looked up and saw her classmates staring at her.

"WHAT ARE YOU STARING AT, BOOGER EATERS??!!!" Destiny pushed with all her might and knocked her desk over. She stood up and stalked out of the room.

Ms. Watts followed her out and closed the door. "That was totally uncalled for, Destiny," she said, standing tall and crossing her arms. "You need to go back in there and clean up the mess and apologized to the class." Destiny balled her fists and punched the wall. She leaned against the wall and slid down. Wrapping her arms around her legs, she buried her face against her knees.

"Clean it up yourself, bitch," she mumbled. Ms. Watts clenched her fists and took a deep breath. Without a word, she turned on her heel and went back into the classroom.

A few minutes later, Destiny heard footsteps. They stopped right in front of her. Without looking, she knew it was Mr. Roberts. She gripped her legs harder and squeezed her eyes shut.

He was so annoying, the way he just stood there and waited. She had tried waiting him out in the past, but it never worked. "WHAT?" she said, looking up at him. "Go away and leave me alone."

Mr. Roberts squatted beside her on his heels. Destiny could smell his aftershave. It reminded her of pine trees. He calmly picked at some paint around his fingernails that he'd missed after working on his house the night before. He didn't say a word.

"God! You are so annoying!" Destiny turned her back to him.

Finally, Mr. Roberts gave a low whistle. "Wow, look at the time. It's like water rushing down a river. You can't stop it. Your class will be going to music soon. Do you want them to come out and see you here, or would you like to come with me to my office?"

Destiny took a second to weigh her options. Sighing, she stood and walked down the hall toward Mr. Roberts's office, head down and shoulders slumped.

She flopped into a chair in the corner of the outer office. She tugged her hood as close around her face as she could get it and leaned against the wall. She shut her eyes and fell asleep. Mr. Roberts let her stay there.

Chapter 3

The next day Destiny walked into the classroom to see that her desk was still on the floor, upside down, its contents still strewn about. She picked it up and shoved the contents back inside, not caring where they went. She went through her breakfast routine, shoving as much extra food into the pocket of her oversized green sweatshirt as she thought she could get away with. She kept her hood up over her head and her back to the class.

Instead of putting her head on her desk, she pulled a thick, stubby red pencil out of her pocket and drew pictures of animals on the back of the math paper Ms. Watts gave her.

When Ms. Watts came to check on her, Destiny tried to shove the paper into the desk. Not fooled, Ms. Watts reached inside and pulled the page out and straightened it. "These are wonderful drawings, Destiny. You are quite the artist. I'd like to see you finish the math on the other side first, then you can work on them. OK?" She flipped the paper over and pointed to the first problem.

"Fine," Destiny grumbled. She began working on the math while Ms. Watts watched. It was multiplication. Destiny hated multiplication. She wrote some numbers on the paper, hoping the teacher would walk away.

Ms. Watts came down to her level. "Hold on a second, Destiny. Let me show you how to tackle this in a different way. I can see you are confusing the steps." She demonstrated the method the class was working on. Destiny sat back and crossed her arms. She didn't even look at the page.

"Now you try," Ms. Watts said, smiling warmly. Destiny picked up the pencil and wrote some more numbers.

"Not quite. Let me show you again," Ms. Watts said. She held out her hand for the pencil.

Destiny gripped the paper in both hands and ripped it in half. She screamed as she shredded it, "THIS IS STUPID. I HATE MATH AND I HATE YOU! JUST LEAVE ME ALONE!" She threw the pieces at Ms. Watts, slammed her chair backward and ran from the room.

She ran down the hall and out the doors. Once on the playground, she climbed up to her spot at the top of the jungle gym. Her eyes were wide and her breath was shallow. The wind blew her matted hair across her face.

Mr. Roberts came outside and looked around. Spotting Destiny, he crossed the blacktop and stood at the base of the jungle gym. He put his hands on his hips and squinted up at her. A sigh escaped his lips as he pushed his glasses up his nose.

They went through the now familiar routine, Mr. Roberts waiting patiently for the anger to work its way out of her system, Destiny perching like a raptor looking for prey. When they finally made it back to his office, Mr. Roberts looked at this small child with dirt smudges on her cheeks, dark circles under her eyes, and shook his head. He glanced at the pictures of his family on his desk; his daughter's high school graduation, his son at the Special Olympics.

"Destiny, this is the third time this week you've been in my office for your behavior. It's like the bees returning to the hive, but there's no honey. What's up?" He spoke softly and calmly.

Destiny pulled her hood over her head and crossed her arms. She refused to look at him and sank lower into the chair.

Mr. Roberts changed tactics. He pulled open a drawer in his desk and pulled out a small plastic pumpkin. He pulled off the top and held it out to her. "Chocolate?"

She didn't move a muscle.

"You know, this chocolate is a lot like you," he said, unwrapping a piece and popping it into his mouth. Destiny closed her eyes and shifted her body away from him. "It comes in a wrapper that you have to peel open. But once you do, there's something sweet inside."

"Shut up," Destiny snarled. "I hate this place. I hate you. I wish you would just leave me alone." She pulled the hood further down to cover her eyes and pulled her knees up to her chest. She tucked her hands into her pocket. She found her stubby red pencil and rubbed it with her thumb.

Mr. Roberts put the lid back on the candy jar and slid the drawer closed. He let Destiny sit there quietly while he worked at his computer. Every once in a while, he looked at her out of the corner of his eye. Slowly she unwound her body and sat up. He continued to ignore her until he saw her feet touch the ground. "Ready to talk?" he asked.

She shrugged her shoulders and stared at the ground.

"Ms. Watts was helping you with your math," Mr. Roberts started. "She was showing you how to solve the problem and..." He paused.

Destiny rubbed her pencil some more. She shrugged her shoulders again and pushed her hair out of her eyes. Her toe traced the pattern on the rug under her chair. "It's too hard," she said. "I can't do it."

"And you didn't want to look dumb in class," Mr. Roberts said. Destiny nodded faintly. "Gotcha."

Mr. Roberts lifted a sheet of paper off his desk. "Ms. Watts gave me an extra copy of the math. How about we tackle it together, just you and me?"

Destiny looked at her fingernails and gave her signature shrug. "Whatever."

For the next ten minutes, she listened and watched as Mr. Roberts explained the math. He solved the first problem, then passed the pencil to her. Destiny wrote down the numbers as he explained the steps. By the time they reached the end of the page, she was solving most of the problems on her own.

They walked back to class together and showed the work to Ms. Watts. She smiled and praised Destiny's work.

"Sorry about what I said before," Destiny mumbled. She went over to her desk and picked up the shredded math paper.

The rest of the day she sat at her seat. She worked on her assignments. She continued to ignore the other students but managed to make it to the end of the day without any more outbursts.

When the bell rang the other students gathered their backpacks, lined up and said good-bye to Ms. Watts. When Ms. Watts turned back to the classroom, she saw Destiny kneeling on the floor, surrounded by the contents of her desk.

"What are you doing?" Ms. Watts asked, confused. "The bell rang. It's time for you to go home."

Destiny didn't look up. She reached inside her desk and pulled out another handful of papers. "I need to clean my desk," she said.

Ms. Watts said, "This can wait until tomorrow, Destiny." She furrowed her brow. "I have a lot of work to do. You should get going."

"It will only take a minute," Destiny said, continuing to empty the contents onto the floor. Soon she was surrounded by the mess. She slowly put the textbooks back inside and then began taking small handfuls of old papers to the trash. Ms. Watts retreated to her desk and was grading papers. She watched Destiny make a show of organizing her belongings and straightening her desk and chair.

"Is there anything you want me to clean for you, Ms. Watts?" Destiny asked, walking up to Ms. Watts' desk. She had her hands in her pocket, rubbing her pencil.

Ms. Watts smiled and shook her head. She capped her pen and said,

"No, Destiny, I'm fine. Thanks for asking. Now it's time for you to leave. I have a staff meeting to get to. Your family will be wondering where you are if you don't get going." She stood and walked with Destiny out of the classroom and down the hall.

As Ms. Watts watched Destiny walk through the big glass door, another teacher walked up. "I don't know why you are so nice to her. Not after the way she treats you."

Ms. Watts said, "You never know what someone is going through. She just needs to know that someone cares for her." She turned and headed to the office.

Chapter 4

Destiny didn't head home. She walked down the street away from the school. There was a small convenience store a few blocks away. She turned down the alley behind the store. By the back door of the store, there were stacks of crates and empty boxes. Methodically, Destiny looked in and behind each one. The door opened suddenly, and Destiny jumped. She started to walk away quickly.

"Yo! Destiny!" She turned around. The clerk from the store motioned for her to come back. "How you been? Haven't seen you around much." The tall young man lit a cigarette.

"Hey, Hector," Destiny said.

Hector leaned against the building and Destiny joined him. They stood there in companionable silence for a few minutes. "I didn't save anything for you today. Didn't think you were coming back."

"That's OK. See you around," Destiny said.

"I'll save you some bread next week, Lil D," Hector said. He flicked his stub into the alley and opened the door. Destiny waved and walked up the alley.

She wandered up the street, kicking an empty cup until she came to a large park. She walked over to the swing set and sat down. She watched a family playing soccer. She scuffed her feet in the dirt. When a group of children came running toward the swings, she got up and moved off. She sat under a tree and leaned her back against the rough bark. She watched the kids play and laugh and run and felt nothing.

She sat there until the park was empty. Until the sun had gone down and taken the shadows with it. Until she thought it might be safe to go home. Home. That was laughable. To Destiny, such a place did not exist. In her mind, the place she went to every night wasn't home, it was just a place to sleep, to get out of the weather.

She considered finding another sleeping arrangement, but the night was growing colder and clouds had formed overhead that looked ominous. She had slept under pine trees, in parked cars, even in ditches before. Her favorite place, though, was up in the trees. She was good at climbing and had found an old cottonwood that had a huge trunk. She had made a kind of treehouse in the crook of its branches. She could see for miles up there and feel the wind on her face.

As she walked, she scanned the ground constantly. You never knew what you might find in the weeds. One time she had found a wallet with five dollars in it. She'd taken it to a fast-food restaurant and bought a bunch of burgers. Ever since then she was always on the lookout for treasures.

Chapter 5

D estiny lived on the last street, in the last row, the last house in the neighborhood. It was one of those places where there were two houses stuck together side by side. Hers was the door on the right. Most of the windows were covered with cardboard. There was very little paint left on the outside. It was as grey as the sky at dusk. The yard was a mess of tall weeds. As Destiny approached it, she slowed her pace. She skirted around the piles of trash and weeds in the front yard. She looked for lights on in the house. One light, good; two lights, bad.

There was light coming from the living room, and some light seeping around the carboard where the kitchen window used to be. Mom was home. So was someone else. She stopped moving. There was an old, white, beat-up truck out front. More bad news, her mother's new deadbeat boyfriend. For a split second, she considered heading to her treehouse. But then a blast of cold fall air hit her and made up her mind. She changed her course and headed around to the back of the house.

Destiny pushed past the broken boards of the fence and walked across the hard-packed earth that made up the back yard. She sat down on the crooked steps leading to the back door. She leaned against the house and watched the stars appear and disappear in the sky between the scudding clouds, listening for sounds coming from inside the house.

She felt something touch her leg. She looked down. Staring up at her hopefully was an orange tabby cat she had named Fur Ball. Destiny reached down and ran her hand over the cat's head. She was rewarded with a small "meow" and a lot of purring. She put her hand deep in her pocket and pulled out a muffin that she had taken from school. Pinching off a chunk, she placed it on the steps. Fur Ball sniffed the food, sat down and nibbled daintily on its dinner. Destiny took a bite and watched the cat. This was the only company that she enjoyed. Fur Ball didn't ask her questions or make her do math problems. Fur Ball didn't scream at her, "Where have you been, you little ungrateful pig!" Fur Ball didn't kick her or call her names like 'Disgusting Dummy'. She could tell Bur Ball anything, not that she did.

The sound of yelling made her jump. Fur Ball took off like a shot. Inside the house, a man's voice grew louder. Something hit the wall and broke. Destiny couldn't make out the words but knew them just the same. Now her mom's voice, just as loud, just as angry. Stomping feet, a slamming door. The roar of a truck engine, squealing tires.

Destiny blew out the breath she had been holding. She was glad for the darkness. Glad for the wall between her and the chaos. She stayed on the steps, waiting for the last shreds of the storm to blow over. She knew if she went inside now, she would bear the brunt of her mother's anger. Better to wait it out. Destiny closed her eyes and turned on her imagination.

She imagined it was summer. She was sitting in the backyard of a different house – her 'real' house – sipping on a glass of lemonade. Her feet were dangling in the pool. She looked over at her mom, wearing a flower print summer dress, relaxing on one of those covered swings, reading a book. Mom looked up and smiled at her. On the patio was a man wearing shorts and a t-shirt. He was cooking burgers on a grill.

The back door opened and light spilled into the darkness. Destiny jumped. Her mother stood there in an oversized t-shirt with a cartoon character on it and smudged black leggings. A cigarette dangled from her lips. Her hair was limp and dirty. She looked at Destiny and scowled. "There you are, you little freak. Get inside."

Destiny scooted past her mother, trying not to touch her. Trying to make herself small. She kept her eyes down. At least her mom wasn't yelling - yet. She managed to get inside without a smack. She hurried through the living room, skirting around the broken-down couch with the stuffing coming out and the coffee table covered in cigarette butts and empty pizza boxes. She made her way down the dark hallway and into her bedroom at the very back of the house. She would have shut the door if there had been one. The victim of an attack from one of her mother's fits.

Turning on the light, she walked over to the wall that adjoined the house next door. Sometimes she found little holes in the wall that the neighbor had drilled to be able to see into her room. She stuffed the holes full of toilet paper and anything else she could find. Satisfied that she had found them all, she walked over to her bed.

Technically, it was just a mattress on the floor. Stained, lumpy, small. But at least it was all hers. She sat down and picked up the orange and blue blanket that was wadded up in the middle. She wrapped it around herself tightly. Looking at the doorway, she paused, then reached under the mattress and pulled out a spiral notebook.

Scooting back until she could lean on the wall, Destiny opened the notebook and flipped slowly through it. Pictures of birds, dogs, flowers, cars, faces, and wild animals covered the pages. Finding a blank page, she stopped.

She put her hand into her deep pocket and pulled out her pencil. Her red, stubby pencil. Her drawing pencil. Slowly and carefully she began outlining the shape of a cat. Fur Ball. Sitting on the back steps. Waiting for her. Looking for her. Wanting her.

Chapter 6

Saturday. Destiny woke early. She opened her eyes slowly and looked around. Her room was cold, but she was used to it. She sat up and listened. She could hear her mother's steady breathing coming from the room across the hall. Standing up, she picked up her shoes and notebook and walked to the door. She had slept in her clothes, like always.

Weekends were hard. At least school was warm and safe, and there was food. Weekends were nothing but cold and pain. Her mother yelled at her. A lot. If she was around. Often, her mother would stay out drinking and partying with her friends and not come home at all. Destiny would be home alone for days at a time. That was hard. Having her mother home was harder. Being alone was the better option. But there was no telling when her mother would return, in what mood, and with whom.

She found it easier just to not be there at all. Standing in the doorway of her bedroom she listened to her mother's breathing. Destiny held her breath and counted to five. Then she tiptoed down the dark hallway to the living room. Avoiding the piles of beer cans, she made her way to the front door.

Destiny turned the knob and slowly pulled the door open. She had learned just how far she could open it before the hinges squeaked. Slipping her slim body through the opening, she turned and eased the

door shut. Only then did she let out her breath. She was surprised to
see a cloud of steam. The ground was covered with a fresh skiff of snow.
She quickly put on her ratty tennis shoes and walked up the street. The
fresh air cheered her, but only a little. She shivered and stuffed her
hands into her pocket.

Sharp hunger pangs struck her. Her small store of food from school
was gone. The brown grass under the snow crunched when Destiny took
a short cut across someone's lawn. There was a fast-food restaurant
not far from her house. She could smell bacon and eggs and pancakes.
She didn't have to check her pockets to know that there was no money,
but she hoped to score something anyway.

The warmth of the restaurant hit her like a wave when she opened
the door. She stepped inside quickly and looked around. There weren't
very many customers. She saw an old couple in the corner. Walking
over to them, she said, "Can I have a dollar?" The man looked her up
and down. "Get lost," he said and turned his back to her.

She turned to a man wearing an orange construction vest over his
coat sitting at a counter. "Do you have any spare change?" she asked.
He glared at her and then took a bite and chewed slowly. She took the
hint and moved on.

A woman pushing a broom stopped her. "Get out of here. We don't
like beggars." She grabbed Destiny's elbow and drug her to the door.

Destiny jerked her arm away. "Let go of me!"

Having no choice, she walked out the door. She tried very hard not to
cry. Her stomach hurt. Her pride was hurt. She tried hard to pretend
that it didn't matter, that THEY didn't matter. Sinking to the cement,
she hugged her knees and buried her head.

It was cold sitting there on the cement. It seeped up through her
clothes and into her bones. She tried to ignore it, but soon she began
to shiver. Her stomach growled and ached. It was getting very hard to
ignore. She was used to it, it seemed to be happening more and more

frequently. She decided to go try her luck at the convenience store. Hopefully, Hector was working today.

Just as she was pushing herself to her feet, a familiar voice called her name.

"Destiny? Is that you?"

Destiny pushed the hood of her sweatshirt back and looked up into the confused face of her teacher, Ms. Watts. Ms. Watts had one hand on the door to the restaurant, the other holding a little girl's hand. They were both dressed in jeans and puffy blue winter coats.

"Oh, hi, Ms. Watts." No use pretending she didn't know her. This teacher could be so annoying. She never left Destiny alone or minded her own business. Her honey-sweet voice made it sound like she cared, but Destiny knew she was just like all the other teachers – it was just her job.

"What are you doing here? Where is your family?" Ms. Watts looked around the parking lot.

Destiny stuffed her hands into her pocket and rubbed her pencil. "I'm...um...just waiting for my mom to part the car. She went around the other side." She looked down at her torn shoes as she talked. She shivered.

"I'll tell you what," Ms. Watts said with a bright smile. "It's too cold out here to wait. Come inside with us." She opened the door and waited.

Destiny didn't know what to do. The people inside would make a huge scene if they saw her come in again. Her heart raced. Her stomach cramped as the breakfast smells wafted through the open doorway. That decided it for her. "OK," she said. She slipped through the doorway, avoiding contact with Ms. Watts, and stepped to the side. Then she followed Ms. Watts and the little girl to the counter, head down, hoping that the lady with the broom wouldn't see her.

Ms. Watts was talking, trying to draw Destiny out of her shell. "Do you have plans for the weekend, Destiny? Are you doing anything special with your family?"

Destiny shook her head. "No. We just stay home most of the time." She didn't want her teacher to know, didn't want anyone to know, what her life was really like.

"Same with us. This is my daughter Isabelle. She was craving a biscuit sandwich this morning. Isabelle, say hello to Destiny. She's one of my students." The little girl peeked around her mother's leg and waved at Destiny. She had sky blue eyes and pink cheeks. Her silky blonde hair was caught up in two ponytails held by pink bows. "She's only two. She's a little shy around people she doesn't know. Give her a few minutes and she'll talk your leg off."

Destiny started to wave back at Isabelle. She noticed the dirt under her fingernails and stuffed her hand quickly back into her pocket. She remembered a time when her mother would play with her hair and put little barrettes shaped like flowers in it. She remembered holding her mother's hand.

Destiny knew that Ms. Watts was going to ask about her mother again. She started backing up and looking toward the door. Ms. Watt put a hand on her shoulder. "Your mother doesn't seem to be here. Are you sure she's parking the car?" A look of concern crossed her face. Her forehead wrinkled in that way teachers have when they know you aren't telling the truth.

The look vanished as quickly as it came. Ms. Watts smiled brightly. "I have an idea. Why don't I buy you breakfast and you can help me keep Isabelle company for a while?" Without waiting for Destiny to answer, she turned back to the counter, keeping her hand on Destiny's shoulder. "We'll have 3 of your Mega Breakfasts, please. And throw in 2 extra biscuit sandwiches, too." She pulled her wallet from her pocket and handed the clerk some money.

She ushered the girls over to a booth by the window and they all sat down. Soon their food arrived. Destiny couldn't get over how much there was. Large glasses of juice, sausage and eggs, pancakes, biscuits, and bacon.

"Here, Destiny, eat this," Ms. Watts said. She put a plate in front of Destiny that was loaded with scrambled eggs and pancakes. "It's going to get cold." Destiny picked up a fork and took a bite. The eggs were light and fluffy, the pancakes were sweet and melted on her tongue. She had never tasted anything so good. Before long, her plate was empty. She had never felt so full.

Ms. Watts kept a stream of comments flowing, trying to draw Destiny into a conversation. Destiny nodded and shrugged and kept her eyes on the table. She shifted in her seat and finally looked around at the door.

Ms. Watts took the cue and said, "Well, Destiny, this has been nice. Isabelle seems to have gotten her fill. It's time I take her home." There was still a lot of uneaten food on the table. Ms. Watts packed it up in a large bag. Then they all made their way out into the cold morning.

"Thanks for the food," Destiny said. She started to walk down the sidewalk.

Ms. Watts said, "Wait! Destiny, it's too cold out here to walk home. Hop in and I'll give you a ride." She said it as a statement, not a question. Little Isabelle ran over and grabbed Destiny's hand.

"Come," she said, tugging.

Ms. Watts smiled. "See, Isabelle wants you to come, too."

Relenting, Destiny allowed the little girl to pull her over to a green Honda. There was a bumper sticker on the back window that said 'I ran Boston 26.2'. Ms. Watts unlocked the doors and helped Isabelle into her car seat in the back. Destiny stood there watching. Ms. Watts then opened the front door and motioned for Destiny to get in.

"Buckle up, please," Ms. Watts said, in her sing-song teacher's voice. Destiny did as she was told.

Ms. Watts turned to Destiny. "Where to?"

There was no way that Destiny wanted her teacher to take her to her house. "Go that way," she said, pointing to the left. "It's not far from here." She directed Ms. Watts to a neighborhood close to the school.

"You can let me out here," Destiny said, pointing to a small green house with a white door. There were kids' toys scattered around the front yard and a black truck in the driveway.

"This is your house?" Ms. Watts asked. She scanned the toys in the yard and noted how they were for toddlers.

"No," Destiny said. She unbuckled herself and opened the door. "It belongs to my aunt. I stay with her sometimes." She stepped out quickly and shut the door. "Well, bye!"

Ms. Watts rolled down the window. "Destiny, wait. Please take the rest of the breakfast with you. We bought way too much this morning." She handed her the bag and drove off slowly, watching Destiny through the rearview mirror. Destiny just stood on the sidewalk, not moving, until the car went around the corner.

Chapter 7

Monday. Back to the routine. Destiny walked slowly up the dirt path by the ditch. Her breath was visible again on this frosty morning. She pretended she was smoking, making her breath come out in big puffs. The snow from Saturday was gone, but the ground was hard.

Just as Destiny reached the sand on the playground, the bell rang. She pushed her way into the building and reached her classroom before the other students. She grabbed a handful of packaged pancakes and shoved them into her pocket. Her classmates came in behind her and she pretended that she had just arrived, picking up more food and carrying it to her desk.

Carefully, she pulled her battered notebook from her pocket and opened it to the page where she had been drawing Fur Ball. As she ate, she started adding details to Fur Ball's face. Morning announcements came and went, the Pledge of Allegiance was recited. Destiny ignored it all. She worked very hard at being invisible in this place.

Just as Ms. Watts began the math lesson, the phone rang. After a brief conversation, she hung up and walked over to Destiny's desk. Destiny jumped when she felt Ms. Watts' hand on her shoulder. She covered her notebook with her arm and looked up. Ms. Watts was standing there with her serious face. Her eyebrows were pulled down and little wrinkles crossed her forehead.

"The office called. Mr. Roberts would like to see you, Destiny," she said softly. The look on her face told Destiny that something was wrong. Blood started pumping in her ears. She shoved the notebook into her pocket and stood up.

"But I didn't do anything, I swear," she said. "God! I hate this place." She felt around in her pocket for her little red pencil and rubbed it furiously.

Ms. Watts tried to rub Destiny's arm. Destiny jerked away. She knew that the other kids had stopped working and were staring at her. She flipped her middle finger at them as she stormed out of the room and down the hall. The hallway between Room 16 and the office seemed to stretch on forever. Her shoes felt like they were made of cement. When she got to the main office, she threw herself into a chair in front of the secretary's desk and slouched down. She kept her eyes on the spot in the carpet where it had been patched. The colors didn't match. She sat there for about 5 minutes until the door to Mr. Roberts's office opened.

"Destiny, there's someone here to see you. You aren't in trouble," he said gesturing to her. Destiny stood up slowly and shuffled towards him. He stepped to the side to allow her to enter his cramped office ahead of him. She crossed the threshold and stopped suddenly. There was another person in the office. She took a step back and ran into Mr. Roberts.

Sitting on one of the chairs was a thin woman with brown curly hair. She was wearing grey slacks and a blue blouse. She stood up when she saw Destiny.

Mr. Roberts said, "I'd like you to meet my friend Miss Laura. She's here to visit with you." His voice sounded loud in the small space like he was forcing himself to be cheerful. He put a hand on Destiny's shoulder. Destiny took a couple of stumbling steps and stopped. Mr. Roberts closed the door gently and went to sit at his desk.

Destiny looked around the office, anywhere but at Miss Laura. Mr.

Roberts's big brown desk took up most of the room. A floor-to-ceiling bookcase took up one whole wall. It was filled with books and binders of all sizes. The piles of papers on his desk had grown larger since the last time she'd been in there.

The woman reached out her hand toward Destiny. "It's nice to meet you, Destiny. Why don't we sit down?"

Destiny furrowed her brow. She clenched her jaw. Her thumb furiously rubbed the pencil in her pocket. She still refused to look at the woman. She fell heavily into one of the padded chairs next to Mr. Roberts' desk and looked at her dirty, scuffed shoes. Laura sat next to her.

Destiny glanced sideways at Miss Laura. Her curly brown hair reached her shoulders. Her eyes were sparkly green and had little lines around them. Her teeth were straight and very white. Her smile was wide.

"As Mr. Roberts said, I'm Miss Laura. I work at Social Services. Have you ever heard of Social Services?"

Destiny nodded slightly.

"What do you know about it?" Laura asked. She tucked a strand of hair behind her ear.

Shrugging, Destiny said, "I dunno. They help kids, I guess."

"Yes, we do help kids. My job is to talk to kids at schools. I talk to kids all day about things that worry them." She looked over at Mr. Roberts and raised an eyebrow.

Mr. Roberts said, "I think of myself as a big bear, Destiny, and you are one of my cubs. I protect my cubs. Miss Laura is one of the people who help me protect my cubs. Please talk to her. I'm going to step out and give you two some privacy." He stood up and moved to the door.

When he had gone, Laura continued, "The reason I am here is that someone had concerns about you. Do you have concerns about you?"

Destiny didn't say anything.

Reaching into the black bag next to her chair, Laura asked, "Do you like to draw?" She put a sketch pad on her lap with a yellow pencil and flipped it open to a blank page.

The only paper Destiny had ever drawn on was notebook paper with blue lines. She eyed the smooth white paper and her fingers twitched. "Yeah, I like to draw."

"Would you be willing to draw some pictures for me?" Laura asked, holding out the notepad.

Destiny took the paper and nodded.

"Great! I want you to draw me a picture of your house of good. What I mean is, draw a picture of everything good in your house."

Destiny glanced at Miss Laura and then at the paper. She quickly sketched an outline of her house and then paused. What was good at her house? She drew her bedroom and her bed. She drew the backyard and Fur Ball, the cat. She handed the paper back to Miss Laura.

"Tell me about this picture," Laura said.

Destiny shrugged. "That's my house, my room, and a cat that hangs around."

"What people in your house are good?" Laura probed gently.

"I don't know. My mom, I guess," Destiny said. "As long as her boyfriends aren't around, she's OK."

Laura asked, "Does anyone else live there?"

Destiny shook her head. "Just me and mom, mostly."

"What do you mean, mostly?"

"Sometimes she lets people crash on our couch, or her boyfriend sleeps over."

Laura nodded and flipped to a new page in the notebook. "Would you draw me another picture? This one is your house of worries. What do you worry about, Destiny?"

Destiny took the pencil and paper and began to sketch. Laura watched quietly. This drawing took longer.

When Destiny handed her the notebook, Laura took a moment to study it. Pointing at a part of the picture showing a man bending over by a wall, she said, "Tell me about this part."

Destiny said, "That's my neighbor. He pokes holes in my room to spy on me."

Laura nodded her head and pointed to another part where another man was standing outside the house, pointing and his mouth was open. "Who is this person?"

"That's our landlord, telling us we have to leave."

"Have you moved around a lot?"

Destiny said, "Sometimes. We've been at this place for a while now. Mom always seems to find ways to get him off our back."

Pointing to another part showing two people next to a couch, Laura asked, "And these people?"

"My mom and her new boyfriend, fighting."

"What do they fight about?" Laura asked.

"Everything."

"What do you hear them say?" Laura probed.

"I dunno. Stuff about money, mostly. She gets mad when they mooch off her too much."

"Do they ever involve you in their arguments?"

Destiny said, "They used to. Now, I just leave so I don't have to hear them."

"How long do you stay away?"

Destiny shifted in her seat. "I come home after dark most days. They usually either make up or he leaves by then."

"Where do you go when you leave?"

"Out. I walk around. I sort of have a treehouse. If it gets cold, I stay in the shed in the back yard." Destiny picked at some skin on her finger.

Laura flipped to another page and handed it back to Destiny. "Could you draw one more picture? Draw your house of hopes and dreams. If you had a magic wand, what would your house be like?"

Destiny thought for a minute. Then she drew a simple sketch. In it were her mother, a small house, a car and her, standing in the front yard. "I wish things could go back to the way they were when I was little," was all she would say.

Laura nodded again. "What did you eat for breakfast this morning?"

"Pancakes and juice."

"What about dinner last night?"

Destiny squirmed in her seat. "Um…" She looked up at Laura's face. "I don't remember."

"Are you ever afraid, Destiny?" Laura asked.

Destiny put her hands back into her pocket. Finding her pencil, she gripped it tightly. "Sometimes, I guess."

"What makes you afraid or worried?"

Destiny dug her toe into the carpet. "I dunno."

"I know that someone has a worry about you not having food to eat at home," Laura shared.

"Yeah, I worry about eating, especially on the weekends," Destiny admitted.

Laura said, "Do you worry about anything else?"

"Sometimes I worry about my mom," Destiny said.

"What do you mean?"

"Like when she has guys over and they be mean to her."

"Mean? How?" Laura probed.

"Like hitting her and yelling. She hits them and yells, too. Sometimes they throw things."

"Do they hit you?"

"Not so much anymore. I get out of there."

"Do you have anyone you can go to when they start fighting?"

"No. I don't know anyone else."

"Destiny," Laura said, closing her notebook, "I am going to go out to your house and talk with your mother today. I want you to know that you might be going to live somewhere else for a while."

Destiny felt a tingle of dread in her stomach.

Chapter 8

Destiny sat in Miss Laura's office. It was even smaller than Mr. Roberts'. The desk was overflowing with papers. The pale blue walls had calendars and sticky notes plastered on them. The only advantage her office had was a window. Granted, it only looked down onto a parking lot and a highway, but hey, at least there was more light.

She counted the ceiling tiles (there were 58), the books on the bookshelf in the corner (44). She thought about getting up and walking out. When she went to the door, there were a lot of people coming and going and sitting in the waiting area. She decided against it and walked back over to her seat. She sat heavily and sighed. Where had Miss Laura gone? What was taking so long? Why was she even here? She sighed again and swung her legs.

At the end of the school day, Destiny had been called back down to the office. Miss Laura was waiting for her. "Destiny, you will not be going home today. Instead, you will be going to your grandparents' house. How does that sound?"

"I don't have any grandparents," Destiny said, shaking her head.

Laura said, "You do have grandparents. Mr. and Mrs. Murphy are your mother's parents. They will be taking care of you for a while."

They walked out of the building and got into Laura's red SUV. Destiny watched out the window as they passed tall buildings and big trees. They crossed a highway and pulled up in front of a tall building with lots of big windows. Destiny had never been in an elevator before. When the shiny silver doors had slid open, she stood still, confused. Laura had to coax her inside. The small, close space made Destiny nervous. She looked around with wide eyes. When the elevator started moving, she backed into the corner.

It was cold in Laura's office, too. Destiny shivered and pulled her notebook from her pocket. She started to draw. She had finished the picture of Fur Ball that morning. Now she sketched the potted plant that was on the window sill. It was a strange kind of flower that had a long, thin stem that curved at the top. The flower only had three petals and was the palest pink. She wished she had some colored pencils.

Hearing the click, click, click of heels on the tile floor outside, Destiny stuffed the notebook back into her pocket and looked up. Laura came bustling into the room. She sat down in her brown leather chair and swiveled it around to face Destiny.

"Your grandparents are on their way. They will be here in an hour. Are you hungry? Let's go get something to eat." She stood up and walked to the doorway. When Destiny just sat there, she motioned for her to stand up. Destiny walked past her, careful not to touch Miss Laura.

Laura and Destiny walked down the street to a nearby restaurant. It was a small place, but clean. There were booths along both side walls and tables in the middle. They sat in one of the booths. The red vinyl seat was overstuffed and bouncy. Laura said, "You can order anything you like. I've eaten here many times and everything I've had has been delicious. They make it all from scratch."

Destiny stared at the menu. Most of the items on it she had never heard of. She had never been handed a menu before. She felt uncomfortable sitting in this place with this strange lady. She shifted in her seat and looked around.

Laura sensed her unease. "They have mac 'n' cheese here. It's gooey and tasty. Do you want some?"

Destiny nodded and closed the menu. When the food arrived, she ate quickly, never looking at Laura. In addition to the mac 'n' cheese, Laura had ordered her a glass of lemonade and some garlic breadsticks. Laura didn't even try to have a conversation with Destiny. She simply let her eat in peace. She ate her salad and watched Destiny devour her food.

When the meal was eaten, Laura noted that Destiny's eyelids were drooping, so she quickly paid the bill and led Destiny outside. They walked back to the office.

When they reached their floor, Destiny was too warm, too full, and too tired to keep her eyes open. They made their way back to Laura's office. She sat in the same chair, leaned back and closed her eyes. Laura took a blanket off a shelf and covered Destiny. She turned off the lights and tiptoed out, shutting the door behind her.

Chapter 9

The day had been a whirlwind of emotions. Confusion, mistrust, fear, anxiety, to name a few. Destiny slept hard until she felt a hand on her shoulder. She jumped up, spilling the blanket to the ground. She looked around wildly, not knowing where she was.

"It's OK, Destiny, it just me," came Laura's voice. "I'm sorry to wake you, but your grandparents are here. It's time to go."

They rode the elevator down to the first floor and went into a small conference room. Destiny stood behind Laura with her hands in her pocket, staring at her shoes. Every once in a while, she glanced up at the couple seated at the table. The man was big and bald. He was wearing jeans and a red and black checkered button-down shirt. The woman was also large. She had short, gray hair and glasses. Her dress had big ugly flowers on it. The woman kept twisting the handle on her purse.

"Destiny, I'd like for you to meet your grandparents, Mr. and Mrs. Murphy," Laura said. The couple stood up and came around the table.

The man stuck his big meaty hand out to Destiny. "Glad to meetcha," he said. "I'm Grandpa Joe. This here's yer Grandma Ida." Destiny shrank away from him.

The woman nodded her head and said, "Yes, dear. It's so nice t' meet ya. We didn't know our Paula had a daughter 'til this lady called us."

Grandpa Joe turned to Laura and said, "Ya sure she belongs to us? She seems mighty skittery. Wouldn't be surprised if she's a runner, like her mom."

Laura led the way out of the conference room and outside. She said to Destiny, "I'll be over in a few days to check on you." Destiny allowed herself to be placed in the back seat of their old faded silver truck. She immediately pulled her hood over her head and turned her face to the window. What else could she do?

Ida kept up a constant flow of chatter on the drive. "Do you like school? What is your favorite subject? Do you like birds? I collect bird figurines, you know." Destiny rolled her eyes and kept her focus on the trees that lined the streets. Joe didn't say a word.

At the end of the trip, they pulled into a driveway next to a house that was as old and faded as the truck. It used to be white, but there were places where the paint had faded out and the brown siding was showing through. The grass was brown and the two trees were bare. There were three bird feeders in one of the trees and a couple of birdhouses hanging from branches in the other one.

They walked into the house and sat Destiny down on an old flowered sofa in the living room. Joe sat heavily in a brown leather recliner in the corner. Ida perched on the sofa next to Destiny. She cleared her throat and picked up a piece of paper that had been lying on the coffee table.

"Here's the rules," Ida said. "I wrote 'em down so's it'd be easy to remember." Joe reached for the remote control. Ida cleared her throat again and he pulled his hand back.

"First," Ida said, reading from the paper, "Ya can call us Joe and Ida. We ain't too formal around here." In her head, Destiny was thinking *your names are Birdbrain and Pops*.

"Next, ya can't touch or play with my china birds," Ida was speaking in her most serious tones. *I'd like to chuck one at your head right now,* thought Destiny.

Ida put down the paper and looked at her. "Are ya listenin'?" She turned to Joe. "Joe, make her take that thing off her head and listen."

Destiny had sunk back on the couch and pulled the hood as far over her head as she could. Her hands were in her pocket, fiddling with her pencil.

"Listen to Ida, girl," Joe said.

Destiny sighed loudly and pushed the hood back on her head. "There. Are you happy now?"

Joe pointed a finger at her. "Watch yer tone."

Ida continued down the list of dos and don'ts. Destiny tuned her out and let her eyes wander around the room. There were bookshelves on either side of the window crammed with porcelain figurines of birds of all sizes and colors. On the walls were framed pictures of Joe and Ida and a young girl that were taken when the couple was much younger. *That must be my mom*, Destiny thought. Finally, Ida stood up and said, "Well, that's it. Let's go look at where ya'll be sleeping."

As they left the living room Destiny heard Joe pick up the remote and turn on the TV to some game show.

Destiny followed Ida up the stairs and into a small bedroom. Ida flipped on the light. There was a bed covered with a brown plaid bedspread that matched the curtains covering the one window in the room. There were a closet and a dresser with three drawers. On top of the dresser were more bird figurines. Some of these were small and delicate. All were made of glass.

"This used to be yer momma's room before she went and ran away. I threw out all her old things. I'm surprised ya don't have a bag of clothes with ya, or a suitcase of some kind," Ida said. "I suppose we'll have to get ya some tomorrow. Can't have ya wearin' the same clothes all the time. Wouldn't look good. I'll leave this list for ya on the dresser. That way ya can look them over and memorize them. Let's get ya in the shower and get ya some dinner."

Ida led the way to the bathroom where, to Destiny's surprise, there wasn't a single bird picture or ornament. It was a plain bathroom. Ida had placed a yellow bathmat on the floor and there were matching towels on the rack. A simple white cup stood next to the sink with a tube of toothpaste and a new toothbrush sticking out of it.

"Take a shower and then come to the kitchen. Yer as filthy as a pig. Didn't yer momma teach ya to bathe? I'll get supper started," Ida finished, closing the door and leaving Destiny standing in the middle of the bathroom.

Destiny had never taken a shower in her life. At home, if she were lucky, she was able to wipe herself down with a rag in a sink full of water. That's if the water was working. After fiddling around with the bright silver knobs, she managed to figure out how to make the water flow from the shower. Taking her clothes off, she stepped in. Feeling the icy cold sting, she jumped back out. She adjusted the levers and cautiously put her hand into the stream. Satisfied that she wouldn't get frozen this time, she stepped in again.

At first, the water kind of hurt. Soon, though, she found that she enjoyed the sensation. Looking down at her feet, she saw rivulets of muddy water streaming towards the drain. There were bottles on the edge of the tub. Destiny inspected them all. She opened them one by one and smelled them. She found a bottle of body wash that smelled like the lilac bushes that stood against the back fence of her school. She had always loved the tiny, pale purple flowers and the scent they gave off in the spring. She poured some into her hand and slathered it over her skin. It felt decadent. She imagined herself as a lilac bush, bees buzzing around her, hummingbirds flitting from flower to flower. She lifted her arms like branches and the shower turned into a rainstorm.

A loud banging on the door brought her back to reality. Joe called through the door, "What's takin' so long in there? Hurry up or supper'll get cold."

Destiny turned off the water and grabbed one of the large towels that were hanging on the rod next to the tub. She quickly dried herself off.

She must have missed some spots when she washed because there were brown streaks on the yellow towel. She reached for her clothes and put them on. Now that she smelled like a lilac bush, she noticed her clothes didn't smell so nice. But she didn't have a choice. They were the only ones she had.

Opening the door, she peeked out. She could hear the couple talking downstairs. Following the sound of their voices, she found her way to the kitchen. Joe and Ida were sitting around a square wooden table set with paper plates and plastic cups that had logos from fast food restaurants on them. In the middle of the table was a large bowl filled with greens and a pizza box.

Destiny's stomach growled. She hadn't realized how hungry she was. She sat down quickly on a chair next to Ida. Ida opened the box and put a piece of pizza on Destiny's plate. She added some salad next to it. Destiny picked up the slice of pizza and devoured it. Ignoring the salad, she reached into the box for another piece.

Joe's hand clamped around her wrist. "Eat your salad first, young lady." Destiny pulled her arm back quickly as if she had been bitten by a snake. Her eyes went wide. She screamed, "Don't touch me!" She jumped up from the table and ran to the living room. She searched for a place to hide. She dove behind Joe's big recliner and curled up into a ball.

She knew what was coming next. Every time she was grabbed and yelled at, a beating followed. That was another reason it was better to be out of the house by yourself when people were around. The sound of scraping chairs on wood was followed by heavy footsteps. Destiny made herself as small as she could.

The footsteps approached the chair and stopped. She could see Joe's shoes. She shivered. The chair shifted and Joe grunted. She looked up. Joe stood there, hands on hips, staring down at her. Suddenly he leaned down and reached for her. Destiny scrambled backward until she ran into the wall. Her blood was rushing in her ears, making it difficult to make out the words he was saying to her. When he moved the chair some more, she stood up and closed her eyes. She balled her hands into fists and raised her arms to protect her face.

"What'cher problem?" Joe said. "Yer actin' like a F'in wild animal. Come out of there, NOW."

Destiny slowly opened her eyes and looked at Joe. He took a step back. His face was red and his jaw was set. He was pointing at the floor next to his feet. She could see Ida standing in the doorway behind him, wringing her hands. Destiny brought her arms down to her sides.

Joe pointed to the stairs. "Get yer butt upstairs and stay there. No goddamn child's gonna run this house. I don't know why we let that woman talk us inta takin' you in."

Destiny ran past him and up the stairs. She closed the bedroom door and climbed into bed.

Destiny lay still under the brown bedspread, listening to the sounds of a strange house. She didn't understand everything that was going on but knew that these people were supposed to watch over her until her mother got her life cleaned up and learned to take better care of her. She couldn't imagine her mother living with these people.

It was dark in the room, but a different dark than she was used to. There was no glow from a street lamp coming through the window. She couldn't hear the creepy man that was her neighbor coughing on the other side of her wall. She couldn't smell stale cigarettes and old pizza. It was very still. If she looked hard, she could see the outline of the closet door on the other side of the room. She heard branches gently knocking on the window. Getting out of bed, she lifted the curtain and stared at the tree closest to the house. For some reason it made her think of Fur Ball. He liked to climb the trees behind her house when he was chasing birds. She wondered what he was doing. Was he sitting on her back steps waiting for her to come and share her food with him? It made her sad, thinking of him there all alone. *He must feel like I abandoned him,* she thought.

Chapter 10

The next morning, Joe banged on Destiny's bedroom door. "Time to get up. Breakfast's ready."

Destiny reluctantly followed him down the stairs. She sat in her chair and watched Ida move around the kitchen. Ida stirred something in a pot on the stove. She wrapped a potholder around the handle and brought it over to the table. Scooping out a large spoonful of a sticky white substance into a bowl, Ida handed it to Joe. Then she did the same for Destiny and herself. She put the pot in the sink and sat down.

Joe handed her a spoon and said, "Don't just set there. Eat before it gets cold." He picked up his spoon and began to eat.

Destiny had never seen anything like this before. It didn't look edible to her. She stuck the tip of her spoon into the glop and tasted it with her tongue. There was no flavor, just hot slime. She put her spoon down.

"What's the matter," Ida asked. "Is the oatmeal too hot for ya? Give it a minute."

Destiny watched the couple as they ate in silence. Every once in a while, Joe would take a slurp of coffee out of an oversized mug that had a picture of a hunting dog on it. She sat on her hands and stayed as still as she could.

Ida said, "Why don't ya try it now. It's cooled down some." Destiny shook her head.

Suddenly, Joe slammed his hand on the table. "Dammit! Eat yer food, ya ungrateful child." Destiny jumped up, ran upstairs into her bedroom and shut the door. She opened the closet door and dove inside.

She heard the door open and steps come across the floor. They stopped at the closet. Ida opened the door and stood there with her hands on her hips. She cleared her throat. "Come out of there. Ya gotta eat. I'll not have that lady sayin' we didn't give ya food."

Destiny turned her face to the wall and ignored Ida. She pulled her hood up and crossed her arms. Her fists were clenched tight. Ida stood there and waited.

"I said come out of there. I'ma count ta three."

Destiny covered her ears with her hands. Suddenly, a viselike hand grabbed her wrist and jerked her upright. "Let me go!" she screamed.

Ida let go and said, "Get to the kitchen, now!" Destiny slouched down the stairs, past the living room where Joe was watching TV and into the kitchen.

Destiny sat at the table and picked up her spoon. Ida had followed her and sat across from her. Tapping the table for emphasis, Ida said, "Eat it all, ya hear? We don't waste no food around here." Putting the spoon into the bowl, Destiny slowly lifted it to her lips. The oatmeal was now cold and even slimier. She put it in her mouth and made a face. She gagged, spit it out, and put down the spoon.

"I'm not eating that junk," she said, pushing the bowl away.

Ida cleared her throat. "Joe, get in here. She's refusin' to eat."

Destiny's eyes went wide and she turned to look into the living room. Joe stood up and slowly made his way to the kitchen table. He put one hand on the table and the other hand on the back of Destiny's neck. He leaned over and put his face close to Destiny. "Do I need to feed ya? If ya don't do what Ida says, there will be hell to pay, believe me."

Destiny leaned away from him. She could smell the coffee on his breath. She wasn't sure what he meant by hell to pay. "Screw you, old man," she said and slid off the chair and around the table. She went back upstairs to her room.

Joe followed her and threw open the door. He hauled her out of the closet and laid her across his knees. With a flat hand, he spanked her bottom three times and then stood her up.

"Ya'll do what yer told," Joe said between clenched teeth. Destiny stared back. Her face was red and her hands were balled into fists.

He stood up and looked at Ida. "Do somethin' about her clothes, will ya? They smell like shit." He went back downstairs into the living room and sat heavily in his chair, turning up the volume on the game show he was watching.

"Why didn't ya bring the rest of your belongin's with ya yesterday?" Ida asked. "Now I have to take you and buy you somethin' else to wear. I didn't know we was goin' to have to spend money on ya. They better get us a check for all this."

Destiny didn't say a word. Finally, Ida gave up and herded Destiny downstairs and went to get her purse.

Destiny followed Ida out to the truck and got in. They drove to another part of town that Destiny had never seen and pulled into the parking lot of a thrift store.

The store was huge. There were rows and rows of clothes hung on racks on one side. On the other side were shelves full of everything you could think of: toys, dishes, books, electronics. In the back, furniture was arranged to look like it was in a house.

They found the children's section and Ida said, "Pick out somethin' to wear." When Destiny hesitated, she said, "Hurry up already. Just grab some clothes." Destiny turned in a circle, not sure where to even start. Most of the clothes she wore she had taken from the lost and found bin at school. She had never been shopping in a real store before.

Ida, frustrated by Destiny's lack of cooperation, reached for the nearest rack and pulled out two shirts and a pair of pants. She pushed

Destiny to the changing rooms to try them on. Destiny went into the small cubicle and did as she was told. It was kind of exciting to get something new to wear. When she came out, Ida sighed, "Ya's a lot skinnier than ya look in that ugly green sweatshirt ya had on. I missed yer size by a lot. Stay here and I'll go find ya somethin' else."

She returned with other clothes. "That's better. I can't be seen with ya lookin' like a homeless person. And ya stink, ya know that? We might as well just burn your old clothes."

She made Destiny wear the new clothes to the checkout stand. They put her old ratty tennis shoes, shirt, and jeans into a bag. When Ida reached for the sweatshirt to put it in the bag, Destiny refused to let go of it. She didn't mind putting her other things into the bag, but the dark green sweatshirt was her security, her armor, her protection from the world. Besides that, the pocket contained her most prized, her only, possessions: her pencil and notebook. She pulled on one side while Ida tugged on the other. "No!" she screamed. Everyone in the store turned to look. "That's mine!" She jerked it away from Ida and hastily put it on over her new clothes. She ran out of the store.

"How dare ya make a scene like that," Ida said storming after her. "I can't believe how bad yer actin'. No wonder yer mamma didn't want ya. Yer just like her. Stubborn and pig-headed. Get in the truck."

The whole way home Ida ranted about how embarrassed she was and how Destiny would pay for what she'd done. Destiny pulled the hood over her head and stared out the window. She made sure that Ida couldn't see the tears that leaked out of her eyes.

As soon as they pulled into the driveway, Destiny opened the door and ran inside. She went straight to her room and slammed the door. It wasn't long before she could hear Ida in the living room rehashing what had happened to Joe. Soon there were two sets of footsteps coming up the stairs. Destiny headed to the closet again.

Joe burst into the room and flung open the closet door. "Come out here and apologize, ya piece a shit," he growled. Destiny turned her back on him. Suddenly she felt herself being lifted by the back of her shirt and hauled into the room. She screamed and kicked and flailed her arms.

"Yer one ungrateful little kid, ya know that?" Joe said. He tightened his grip on the fabric. "Say yer sorry!" He shook Destiny. His face was red and he was panting. He didn't let her go, even when several well-aimed kicks landed on his shins.

"I hate you!" Destiny screamed. "I hate both of you! I never wanted to come here in the first place."

Joe held onto her until she quit kicking and hitting. He pushed her onto the bed. "Ya don't come out of this room 'til I say so." He turned and stomped out of the room, closing the door behind him.

Destiny put her hands into the pocket and pulled out her notebook. She held it to her chest and let herself cry.

A few hours later she heard a knock on her door. She sat up and looked around. She had fallen asleep. She searched frantically for her notebook. There was another knock on the door. She found her notebook on the floor and shoved it under the bed.

She wiped her face with her hands and walked to the door. When she opened it, she was surprised to see Laura standing there.

Laura said, "May I come in?" Destiny nodded and stepped back. Laura came in and stood by the bed. Destiny glanced into the hall. No one was there. She closed the door quickly.

Laura walked around the room for a minute and then sat on the bed.

"Joe called me and asked me to come over," Laura said. "He told me that there were some issues." She stopped and looked at Destiny. Destiny kept her head down and put her hands into her pocket and shrugged her shoulders. It had always been her experience that adults only believed other adults and that they had their minds made up about things before they talked to her.

Laura said, "This is a nice bed." She bounced a little. She stood up and went to the window. Pulling the curtain aside, she said, "Oh, look! Some birds are at the feeder! You must like being up so high, like a treehouse." She looked back at Destiny, who hadn't moved from her place by the door.

Laura wandered over to the dresser and picked up one of the small bird figurines. "Ida really likes birds, doesn't she?" Not getting any response, she returned the object to its place and came back to the bed. "I know this is hard for you, Destiny. You are in a strange place with people you don't know. You are used to being by yourself and having to take care of yourself. That's not the way it's supposed to be for a child. The adults in your life are supposed to take care of you. Your grandparents are trying to do that the best they know how. Give them a chance, will you?"

Destiny pulled her pencil out of her pocket and rubbed it. She refused to look at Laura. The silence grew. Laura rubbed her pants with the palms of her hands.

After another five minutes of silence, Laura stood up and went to the door. "I'll come back tomorrow to check on you, OK?" Destiny didn't even look up to acknowledge her.

Chapter 11

For the next two days, Destiny was left to her own devices. She stayed in her room, only coming out for meals, which she ate in silence and immediately returned to her room. She spent the time drawing in her notebook or looking out the window.

Laura, true to her word had come over to see how she was doing. They had gone outside for a walk around the block.

"This is a nice neighborhood," Laura said.

Destiny said, "I guess." She kicked a rock and watched it bounce into the street.

They walked to the end of the block and found a small park with a playground. They sat side by side on the swings. Destiny dug the toe of her shoe into the dirt and pushed herself back and forth. Laura swayed slightly left and right, holding onto the chains. They sat in companionable silence for a while.

"Where's my mom?" Destiny asked suddenly.

Laura stopped her swing and looked at Destiny. She said, "We don't know. We've been looking for her every day since we brought you here and no one has seen her. I've driven to your house three different times and left notes on the door."

"I want to go home," Destiny said, softly. She looked at Laura. "Can't I just go home? It's not like I was hurting anyone or doing anything wrong. Please take me back there. This place feels like jail."

Laura shook her head. "No can do. Look at it this way. You are warm and safe and clean and have food that you don't have to beg for. Ida and Joe aren't that bad. When your mom gets help and learns how to take care of you, then we will take you back. It could take a while."

Destiny appreciated that Laura was straight up with her. She didn't try to sugar coat anything or beat around the bush. It didn't make her feel any better, though. "Can you at least get them to stop bugging me about my clothes?"

Laura smiled. "I can talk to them about it. It wouldn't hurt to try and meet them halfway. I think that Ida is just a clean freak and wants to wash everything."

They stood up and walked back to the house. Destiny ran up the stairs to her room and shut the door. She could hear voices in the living room and then the front door open and shut. Laura beeped the horn of her car as she pulled away. Destiny stood at the window and watched until her car was out of sight. She turned around and saw her old clothes, clean and folded neatly, sitting at the foot of her bed. She opened one of the dresser drawers and shoved them inside.

After dinner that night, Ida said, "Destiny, after ya help with the dishes, I want ya to go take a shower. Ya haven't cleaned ya'self up since the day ya got here. Ya stink something awful. Wash yer hair, too. I don't want no bugs in this house, ya hear. Ya need to shower every day."

Destiny thought about what Laura had said about meeting Ida halfway and getting her off her back. She cleared the table as quickly as she could, went upstairs and started the shower. She was lathering herself up when she thought she heard the door open and shut. She moved the shower curtain aside and checked. She didn't see anyone. She finished her shower and pulled a towel off the rack. When she dried herself off, she was pleased that this time there weren't any brown streaks on the towel. She stepped out of the tub and froze.

49

All of her clothes were gone. Her new shirt and jeans, her socks and underwear, and her green sweatshirt. A knot formed in her throat and she looked around the small room desperately. Destiny wrapped the towel around herself, flung open the door and ran to her bedroom. She dug out her old clothes and hastily put them on. She looked under the bed, in the closet. Nothing. She stopped and stared around her in disbelief. Then she threw the pillow across the room. She tore off the comforter, the blankets, the sheets. Panic set in. She couldn't find her sweatshirt. All her pent-up fear and anger exploded. Destiny screamed.

Tears flowed from her eyes and blurred her vision. She went back to the dresser and pulled out all the drawers, letting them fall to the floor with a loud bang. She picked up the glass figurines one by one and threw them against the far wall, smashing each one. She was breathing hard. Her heart was thumping, the blood surging in her ears. She tried to lift the mattress but only succeeded in shifting it halfway onto the floor.

Destiny was sobbing and screaming and crying all at the same time. She tore around the room, pulling pictures off the wall, tearing the curtains off their rods.

The door flew open. Ida and Joe came charging in. "What in God's name is going on in here!" Joe yelled. Ida gasped and put her hands to her mouth.

Destiny tried to run past them, but Joe caught her around the waist and held on. Destiny balled her fists and struck out. She kicked and screamed and tried to get away. He held on and pulled her back into the room. He fell back on the mattress and held her.

"Let me go, you filthy pile of shit!" Destiny screamed. "I'll kill you! I swear I will." She bared her teeth and snarled at them. She tried to bite him. She writhed and twisted, but Joe was stronger than she was. After a while, Destiny let her body go limp. Sobs of anger wracked her body and she covered her eyes with her arms.

When Joe felt she had no more fight left in her, he let her go. Panting, he said, "Explain yourself, ya wretched child." He heaved himself up off the floor. "What were ya thinking? Why did ya do this?"

Ida was over by the wall, picking up the broken pieces of glass.

Destiny turned away from him like she always did. She wiped the snot from her nose with the sleeve of her shirt. She started to crawl towards the closet.

"Not this time," Joe said, dragging her back and standing her up.

Destiny tried to move away, but he held her there. "Why did ya do this?" He shoved his face inches from her and raised his voice. "Answer me!" His breath reeked.

She stood there in silence. Her whole body was shaking as her anger started to grow again. "Leave me alone!" she screamed. "I hate you! I hate this place! You stole from me! She stole from me." She pointed a finger at Ida, who was now standing in the doorway, her hands full of broken glass.

"Stole from ya?" We didn't take anythin' from ya. Ya don't have anythin' to steal, anyways." Joe looked at Ida, quizzically. She shrugged her shoulders.

"Liar!" Destiny spat out. "Where is my sweatshirt? It was in the bathroom when I took a shower and now it's gone. You took it! You hate it, so you took it and threw it away! I know you did!" She struggled to get away from Joe.

Ida said, "I didn't take it, ya little monster. I put it in the washing machine. It reeks!" She turned around and left the room.

"Give it back," Destiny cried, wriggling out of Joe's grasp. She managed to make it to the hallway. She pushed Ida out of the way and ran down the stairs. She wasn't sure where the washing machine was, so she tore from room to room, knocking things off surfaces, crashing into things. When she finally found it, she lifted the lid. It was empty.

Screaming, she pounded her fists on the lid. She picked up the bottle of detergent and hurled it against the wall. She threw clothes, shoes, fabric softener, anything she could get her hands on. Joe rushed at her and pinned her arms down. She kicked him in the shins and butted his chest with her head. When she couldn't get free, she stood there and screamed until her voice was hoarse. Ida reached around her, opened the dryer and shoved the green fabric against her face. "Here's your stupid old sweatshirt," she said in a loud and angry voice. "Look what ya done to our home. Yer finished here. I'm calling Miss Laura right now. Ya will not spend another night under this roof." Ida wheeled around and marched off.

Joe let go of her and Destiny picked the sweatshirt up off the floor where Ida had dropped it. She reached into the pocket. Nothing was there. She sank to the floor. Her face went white. "Where are my things?" she croaked. That notebook and pencil were her lifelines. The only things familiar in an unfamiliar world. They kept her grounded, made her feel sane. Now they were gone, missing, ruined by the washing machine. She felt like dying. Everything faded away. She couldn't hear people yelling at her, couldn't see the blue speckled linoleum, couldn't smell the laundry detergent spilled all around her. All she felt was cold. All she could hear was the blood rushing in her ears.

Ida shook her shoulder. "Here, ya little brat. They were on the kitchen counter." She thrust the pencil and notebook against Destiny's chest and marched off.

Chapter 12

When Laura arrived, Destiny was sitting on the couch in the same spot she had sat when she first got there. She was hunched over with her hood up. Joe was sitting in his chair watching a football game.

"Get this kid out of my house," Joe said when he saw Laura. "She's nothin' but trouble with a capital T. Ungrateful, destructive, probably end up in juvie before long."

Ida nodded. "I want her gone. She wrecked the house and broke my birds. Who's gonna pay for it?"

Joe said, "She don't belong in this family. I never want to see her again." He pointed to the door. Ida stood next to his chair, arms crossed, nodding.

Laura didn't say anything to them. She walked over and sat next to Destiny. She leaned close to her and said, "Destiny, I'm taking you with me. Come on, let's go." She stood up and walked to the door. Destiny stood up and followed her.

In the car, Laura turned on the radio. She found a station that played country music and started to sing along. She glanced over at Destiny, slumped against the passenger door, staring out the window, hands tucked far into the pocket of her now clean sweatshirt.

Seeing a fast-food restaurant, she pulled into the drive-through. Laura ordered two burgers with fries and drinks. After she got the food, she pulled into a parking space and shut off the car.

Handing Destiny her food, they sat in silence, eating. Finally, Laura broke the silence with a question. "What happened over there?" She said it quietly, nonjudgmentally. Then she waited expectantly.

Destiny didn't answer. She had no reason to believe that Laura was any different from the other adults in her life. They barely knew each other. Besides, Laura had been the one to put her in that house.

"This is all your fault," Destiny said, finally. She stared at her fries as she talked. She closed her lips into a tight thin line.

Laura opened her eyes wide. She covered her surprise by taking a big drink through her straw. Collecting herself, she said, "I guess you are right, in a way. I trusted them to take care of you." The silence stretched between them. Laura ached to hug Destiny, to say she was sorry, but she knew that Destiny wouldn't believe her. Not yet.

Destiny picked up her last fry and played with it.

"Whatever happened back there must have made you angry. It must have felt like a personal attack on you."

"I thought she stole from me," came the answer, barely audible.

"Stole what?" Laura matched Destiny's voice level.

"My sweatshirt, my pencil, my drawings."

Laura nodded. "I see you have your sweatshirt back. Did you get the other things back, too?"

Destiny nodded and dropped the fry back into the bag. She put her hand into her pocket and pulled out the pencil and notebook. This conversation wasn't going the way Destiny expected. She expected to get a lecture on how she should behave, how wrong it was for her to do what she did, how she should apologize, how much trouble she was in. If it had been her mother sitting here, she would have told Destiny how stupid she was, how she should never have been born.

Instead, Laura just sat and listened. She nodded her head and let the silence grow. Destiny put her notebook and pencil back into the pocket.

The late-night glow of the streetlamp cast a soft light in the car.

"Those things must be important to you," Laura said. She reached up to her neck and pulled out a heart-shaped pendant on a chain. It swung gently, catching the light. "My mother gave me this before she died. It stays with me all the time. If anything ever happened to it, I don't know what I'd do." She tucked it back inside her shirt and patted it. Destiny nodded, watching Laura face.

Destiny looked out the window. "I guess I kinda freaked out back there."

Laura nodded. She started the car and backed out of the parking space.

"What happens now?" Destiny asked. "Am I going back there?" Her big, dark eyes turned to Laura. Her thumb rubbed her pencil, hard.

Laura shook her head. "No, Destiny. You will not go back there. We are going to my office so I can find you a different place to stay."

"Can't you just take me back to my house? I promise I'll be good. I didn't mean to get my mom in trouble. I didn't do it on purpose, I swear!"

"Destiny, you didn't get your mom in trouble. You are too young to be living on your own like you have been doing. We need to get your mom some help so she can take care of you better. Until then, you will have to stay somewhere else."

The drive back to Laura's office was quiet. It wasn't a bad quiet. Laura used her badge and a key code to get into the building. All the lights except the ones over the doors had been turned off. Their footsteps echoed in the empty lobby.

When the elevator dinged and the doors opened, the office furniture cast strange shadows on the floor and walls. Laura flipped on the lights and led Destiny to a couch. She found her a blanket and pillow. "Try to get some sleep. I'll be in my office for a while making phone calls. Come and get me if you need anything."

Destiny laid down and covered herself up. Laura turned off the lights and went to her office. She closed the door most of the way. Destiny lay on her back and stared at the ceiling. She was glad she didn't have to go back with Joe and Ida, but fear started to grow in her that somewhere else might be worse.

Chapter 13

Laura had exhausted all her leads to find Destiny's family. There was no need for a family engagement meeting because Destiny and her mom had no ties to the community. Her parents had kicked Destiny's mom out when they found out their teenage daughter was pregnant.

Paula had severed all ties to her family. They had moved around and kept to themselves. No neighbors or school staff were close to her that could take her in. She decided that maybe a placement where there were other children might be a good idea for Destiny. She would have someone close to her own age to interact with. Maybe it would draw her out of her shell and give her opportunities to act like a regular kid. A few phone calls later, she found what she was looking for. She looked at her watch and sighed. It was past midnight. She walked out to the waiting area and gently woke Destiny.

"Destiny, time to go. I've found a place for you," she said. "Bring the blanket and pillow with you. You can sleep in the car. It's going to be a long drive." This family lived in a different county. It was the best placement she could find. Foster families weren't exactly the most common commodity.

Destiny fell asleep before they had left the city. Laura glanced at her and smiled. Destiny looked so peaceful. She looked like a totally different child; no fear, no worries. *Like a child should look*, she thought to herself. She gripped the steering wheel harder and drew her mouth into a tight line. *Why does life have to be so unfair?*

An hour later they pulled up in front of a big old white two-story house with giant trees in the front yard. Destiny woke up with a start when Laura turned off the engine. She wiped her eyes with the back of her hand. She looked out the window. Lights on either side of the door gave a soft glow to the front porch that wrapped around the sides of the house like a big hug. There were lights on in the first-floor windows, too. Destiny could see rocking chairs in the shadows. The front door opened and a woman came out wearing jeans and a blue cardigan. She came down the steps quickly and stood next to the car.

Laura opened her door and said, "We're here, Destiny." Destiny didn't move. She watched Laura come around the front of the car and shake hands with the woman. Laura was much taller, but the other woman was much thinner. They both came over to Destiny's door. Laura opened it. "Come on out and meet Susan."

Destiny unbuckled herself and slid to the ground. She stuck her hands into her pocket and looked at her shoes.

"Hi, Destiny. I'm Susan Moore. Please come inside. It's too chilly to stand around out here." Her voice was soft and soothing. There was a hint of a southern accent in it.

Laura opened the back door of the SUV and pulled out a small red suitcase on wheels. She handed it to Destiny. "I brought you some more clothes," she said.

They walked up the sidewalk and climbed the steps onto the porch. Susan opened the door wide, but before anyone could go in, a giant fluffy brown dog ran out, jumped up on Destiny and planted a sloppy wet kiss on Destiny's forehead. Destiny shrieked and put her arms up.

"Jackson, get down," Susan said. The dog obeyed and stood there wagging its tail. Its tongue hung out of its mouth.

They managed to navigate around the dog and make their way into the house and then to the living room. There were three couches covered with blankets arranged in a U shape around a fireplace. On the mantle were several framed family photos. There was a formal picture of Susan sitting in a chair with a tall boy on one side and a young girl on the other side. Others were snapshots taken on vacations to the beach, and one of Susan and the kids on a ski slope. Destiny felt small in the big space. She sat in a corner of one of the couches while Laura and Susan talked.

Too soon, Laura turned to Destiny and said, "Good-bye, Destiny. I'll come by sometime tomorrow to check on you."

The red pencil in Destiny's pocket was getting some serious wear by then. There was a lump in Destiny's throat and it was hard to breathe. She had never felt so uncomfortable in her life. She simply nodded at Laura. Susan walked Laura to the door and then came over and sat next to Destiny. Jackson stood next to her, wagging his tail so hard that it banged against the coffee table.

"You must be super scared right now, Destiny. That's OK. I can't imagine what you are thinking. Are you hungry? Thirsty?"

Destiny shook her head.

"Then let's get you settled in bed for the night. I'll pull out the couch and let you sleep down here tonight so we don't wake the kids." While Destiny watched, Susan moved the coffee table, took the cushions off one of the other couches and pulled on a handle. The whole inside came out and turned into a bed. Susan put sheets and blankets on the bed and added some fluffy pillows. She patted the bed and said, "All done! My room is just down the hall. If you need anything, just call. The bathroom is the first door, my room is the second door. Good night, Destiny. I'm so glad you are here."

She turned off all but one lamp, took one last look at Destiny, and walked out of the room. Destiny never took her eyes off of Susan. When she was all alone, she slowly stood up and walked to the bed. Only taking off her shoes, she climbed in between the cool sheets. She pulled the blanket up to her neck. Hearing a loud panting sound, she turned her head. Jackson was sitting next to her with his tongue sticking out. He put his paw on the bed. She scooted over and he jumped up next to her. He lay down and put his paw on her shoulder. She petted him until she fell asleep.

Chapter 14

In the morning, Susan found them snuggled up together with the blankets and sheets twisted in knots. She smiled and tiptoed around the couch to the kitchen. Soon the smell of bacon frying woke Destiny. She sat up and rubbed her eyes. Jackson yawned, stretched and hopped off the bed. Destiny got up and followed him. The kitchen was painted yellow and there were white ruffled curtains framing the window over the large farmhouse sink.

The cabinets were oak and the floor was made of white tile.

Jackson barked softly and Susan turned from the stove. "Good morning, you two. Did you sleep OK, Destiny?"

Destiny nodded. Her stomach grumbled loudly.

Susan laughed. "Sounds like you need some breakfast. It will be done soon."

Loud footsteps came from the direction of the stairs. A tall boy in a t-shirt and jeans with bare feet came into the kitchen. His brown hair was a jumbled mess and there were sleep lines on his face.

"Derrick, meet Destiny. Destiny, this is my oldest child, Derrick. He's thirteen," Susan said, pointing at each of them with her spatula.

"Hi," Derrick mumbled and plopped himself onto one of the chairs around the kitchen table. He poured himself a glass of orange juice and drank the whole thing down in one gulp. He wiped his mouth and poured another glass. He picked up another glass and poured it full.

"Here," he said, holding it out to Destiny.

She took it timidly and stood there staring at him with wide eyes.

"I promise, he can speak in full sentences," Susan said. "Orange juice usually kick starts his brain." She smiled at Derrick and turned back to the stove.

Another, smaller set of footsteps sounded on the stairs. Destiny turned and saw a little girl in a pink sweatshirt and crooked pigtails clutching a doll.

"Good morning, Julie. This is Destiny. She's going to be living with us," Susan said, hugging her daughter. Julie ran up to Destiny and hugged her around the middle, almost causing Destiny to spill the glass of juice she was still holding.

"You are going to share my room! We can play dolls together and have tea parties!" Julie was practically running in place; she was so excited. Destiny didn't know what to make of it. No one had ever been this excited to be around her. She took a step back and looked at Susan.

Susan said, "Settle down, Julie. Can't you see that you are making Destiny uncomfortable?" She turned to Destiny, "She has always wanted a sister. She'll calm down in a minute. Why don't you sit down? Breakfast is ready."

They sat at the round oak table and ate eggs and bacon. Destiny didn't say a word. She watched Susan, Derrick, and Julie carefully. Julie couldn't stop talking. She bounced up and down in her seat and had to be reminded several times to calm down.

As soon as she had put her dishes in the sink, Julie ran to Destiny and tugged on her arm. "Come see our room," Julie urged. "You're gonna love it! It's pink and white and there are two beds and a dollhouse and everything!"

Susan said, "Destiny, would you like to go with Julie to see where you'll be staying? You don't have to if you don't want to go yet."

Destiny decided she would rather go to the pink room than stay in the kitchen with Susan and Derrick, so she let Julie lead her up the wide stairs. Julie kept up a steady stream of chatter as they went. Jackson tagged along, punctuating Julie's statements with an occasional, "Woof!" Every time he did that, Destiny jumped. She had never been around any dog before, much less one that looked like he needed a saddle and live in a barn. Destiny walked slowly, looking at all the pictures that lined the stairs. Most were school pictures from each year. There were a few pictures of an older couple that Destiny guessed were grandparents.

Upstairs, at the end of the long, pale blue hall, Julie flung open a big white door and announced, "Ta-Da!" Sure enough, there was enough pink inside to cover Cinderella's castle. Frilly white curtains covered the large window and the beds were spread with matching pink bedspreads. A desk stood under the window with a pink lamp on it. An enormous dollhouse stood proudly on the opposite wall. Julie patted one of the beds. "This one is yours. That one is mine. We're going to have so much fun!" She climbed up on Destiny's bed and started jumping. Jackson started barking and Destiny stood, frozen, in the doorway with her hands in her pocket.

Suddenly there were hands on her shoulders and she jumped. "Sorry Destiny. I didn't mean to scare you. Julie, get down this minute. You know you aren't supposed to jump on the beds!" Susan went around Destiny and stepped into the room. Susan set the red suitcase from Laura down next to the dresser. She showed Destiny which drawers were hers in the big dresser. "Let's leave Destiny alone for a few minutes so she can put away her things, OK?" She ushered Julie and Jackson out of the room and shut the door.

Destiny unclenched her fists and let go of her pencil. She relaxed her shoulders and looked around. Everything looked brand new. And girly. She had never been a fan of pink. It got dirty too easily. Green was more her style. Her eyes settled on the suitcase. Curiosity got the best of her and she put it on the bed.

Inside there were two unopened packages, one of socks and one of underwear. There was also a new pair of jeans, a heavy jacket, and some tee shirts. Pinned to the jacket was a note from Laura. 'You can do this. You are a strong girl. Laura.'

Destiny unpinned the note and stuck it in her pocket. A tear escaped from her eye and she brushed it away. Then she closed the suitcase and slid it under the bed. She didn't think she'd be here long enough to empty it.

Chapter 15

Susan's philosophy was 'Busy children are happy children'. Destiny was never by herself for long. On Monday, Destiny found herself standing on AstroTurf in an indoor soccer arena. She had put on the cleats Susan bought her, but refused to change into shorts and a t-shirt. She stood in one spot and half-heartedly kicked at the ball if it came near her. The coach was an older man who enjoyed blowing his whistle. After a while, Destiny wandered off the field and sat on a bench.

On Tuesday after school, Susan took Destiny and Julie to the nearby recreation center for swimming lessons. No amount of persuasion could convince Destiny to put on a swimsuit and get into the water. Susan didn't push too hard, and in the end, they sat on the bleachers together and watched Julie splash and play.

Wednesday was piano lessons. The instructor, Darrin, was a young man studying music education at the college. He came to the Moore's house on his motorcycle. Knowing that new things were hard for Destiny, Susan let Julie take her lesson first.

Destiny sat at the kitchen table drawing in her notebook. When the timer went off, Julie skipped over to the table.

"Your turn," she said, leaning on Destiny's arm. Destiny ignored her and kept drawing.

Darrin patted the piano bench. "Come join me, Destiny. I'll show you how to play 'Chop Sticks'. It's one of Julie's favorites." Destiny acted like she didn't hear him.

Susan shook her head. "Maybe she'll be ready next week. See you then, Darrin. Thanks for coming over."

Thursdays were dance classes. Julie was excited that Destiny was going to be in her dance class. When they arrived at the recreation center, she practically dragged Destiny into the dance studio to meet the teacher.

"Miss Carly, Miss Carly! I brought my sister to dance," she said, beaming.

Miss Carly flashed a big smile and swung her wispy blonde hair up into a messy bun. She was tall and slender and moved gracefully across the floor. When she came over to meet Destiny she said, "You will have so much fun with us." Destiny just stood in the middle of the floor, hands in her sweatshirt pocket, staring at the floor.

Two other young girls came into the room and Miss Carly went over to greet them. Julie tugged on Destiny's sleeve and showed her the barre and the mirror. When the tour was over, Destiny found a place in the corner and sat down. She put her hood over her head and ignored the class.

Carly came over and knelt beside her. "Destiny, class is starting. Come and join us."

No response.

Carly tried again. "We really want you to dance with us. Will you, please?"

Nothing. It was like talking to a statue. The other girls were getting wild. She glanced over at them and sighed.

Carly started the class. Every once in a while, she would glance over at Destiny. For the entire class period, Destiny didn't move. She was as still as stone.

When Susan came to pick up the girls, Carly walked over to talk to her.

"Mrs. Moore, I tried to get Destiny to join us, but she refused to even try. She just sat in the corner."

Susan put her hand on Carly's arm. She said, "Just be patient with her. Give her time. Eventually, she'll come out of her shell, I promise."

The next week, Julie and Carly managed to get Destiny to stand by the barre. She didn't participate in the warm-up, but at least she wasn't sitting in the corner. When the class moved to the center of the floor, Carly tried to get Destiny to join in.

"Destiny, come here. I saved this spot for you," she said cheerfully. She smiled her biggest smile. The other girls stopped talking and looked on.

Carly tried again, "Destiny, come join us, please." The girls chimed in.

Destiny ignored them and turned her back.

"Destiny, you are here to learn dance. Come to the floor, now." Carly's tone was still nice, but there was an edge to it. She frowned and brought her eyebrows together.

Destiny shook her head and pulled her hood up. She sat down, turned toward the wall, and pulled her knees to her chest.

Gritting her teeth, Carly walked over and knelt down. She put her hands on Destiny's shoulders and turned her around. Destiny tried to turn away, but the teacher wouldn't let go.

"NO!" Destiny screamed. "Let go of me! Don't touch me!" She pushed Carly, who lost her balance and fell backward. The other girls gasped and ran to the opposite side of the room. They huddled together and watched with wide eyes.

Looking up, Destiny saw everyone watching her, so she scrambled to her feet and ran for the door. She slammed it open and took off down the hall. Susan, who had been sitting in a chair by the front desk, saw Destiny run out, followed by the instructor. She dropped the magazine she was reading and ran after them. Catching up with them in the locker room, she demanded, "What's going on here?" She looked back and forth between the two angry girls.

Carly's face was flushed and she was breathing hard. She pointed a shaky finger at Destiny and said, "She pushed me down!"

Destiny was stiff and her hands were balled into fists. She yelled, "She put her hands on me!" Her eyes were wide and wild.

Susan stepped in between the two. "You," she said, pointing to Carly, "out." Carly spun on her heel and stomped out. "You, sit down," she said, turning to Destiny.

Destiny sat heavily on a bench between the lockers. She crossed her arms and put her chin on her chest. Susan sat next to her. She didn't say anything for several minutes. She glanced sideways at Destiny. Destiny's chest was heaving and her whole body was tense. Susan kept her hands clasped in her lap and her shoulders down. She took deep, even breaths.

After a while, Destiny dropped her own shoulders and Susan noticed that her breathing had slowed a little bit. Destiny glanced over at Susan. She said, "You remind me of Mr. Roberts. Whenever I would get mad, he would sit with me and wait, too."

Susan smiled. "Ready to talk?" she asked softly.

Destiny turned on the bench so that her back was to Susan. "Why should I talk to you about it. You're going to side with her anyway, no matter what I say."

"Try me," came the response. Then silence. Susan let Destiny take her time and knew that eventually she would say something.

The silence was what got to Destiny. She was used to her mother yelling at her, teachers badgering her, asking questions, trying to pry things out of her, getting angry with her when she wouldn't talk. The only person who ever treated her like this was her old principal. Maybe Susan would listen to her.

"What do you want me to say?" she asked Susan. She punched the bench in front of her. She still wouldn't look at her foster mother. "I don't like Carly. She is so fake. She acts like she likes me when you are around, but then when you leave, she's mean." She mimicked Miss Carly's voice, "You are here to dance!"

Susan held her questions in. She took it slow, letting Destiny guide the conversation. She wanted Destiny to know that she was being heard. "You think she's mean. You think she's fake. You really don't like her," she said instead. She kept her voice even and spoke slowly. More waiting.

Finally, Destiny turned around. "Here's the thing. I don't know how to dance. She uses words I don't understand and I feel dumb in front of all those other girls. I'm the biggest one in there. They laugh at me behind my back. I wasn't bothering anyone, but she wouldn't leave me alone."

"She wouldn't leave you alone," Susan repeated.

"Right. She came over to where I was sitting and tried to embarrass me. I know everyone was looking at me. I ignored her, but she wouldn't stop. Then she grabbed me. I told her to stop but she wouldn't. I got angry and pushed her." The last part came out in a rush. She looked up at Susan, expecting to see angry eyes. Instead, she saw caring. "I guess I shouldn't have done that." Destiny hung her head and stared at her feet.

"What do you think you should have done?" Susan asked.

Destiny shrugged and pulled on a loose thread on her sweatshirt. "I should have tried to do what she told me, but I don't know how."

"Or tell her that you didn't understand, maybe," Susan added. "She can't read your mind, Destiny. She obviously assumed that you knew what to do and weren't doing it just to be difficult."

The door to the locker room opened and the girls from the dance class came in, giggling and talking. When they saw Destiny, they stopped. Some of them turned around and left. Others went around the far side

69

of the locker room to avoid her.

Susan stood up. "Destiny, we need to go find Carly and talk to her." Destiny slowly stood up and followed her out into the lobby.

Carly was standing behind the front desk talking to a man wearing a dark suit and a maroon pinstriped shirt unbuttoned at the top. He had dark bags under his eyes and looked like he hadn't slept in a few days. Carly stopped mid-sentence when she saw Susan and Destiny walk up. She crossed her arms and glared.

The man reached over the desk and shook Susan's hand. "Hi, I'm Mr. Garcia. I'm the director of the rec center. Carly was just telling me what happened in her class. Sounds like there was some pushing involved." He frowned at Destiny.

Susan held up a hand. She said, "Is there somewhere private that we could all go to talk? Before we jump to any conclusions, we should hear both sides of the story, don't you think?" She raised her eyebrows at him.

Mr. Garcia nodded his head. "Of course, you're right. My mistake." He looked behind him. "My office is too small to fit us all comfortably. Besides, it looks like a bomb went off in there." He chuckled. "Why don't we go back to the dance studio. There aren't any more classes today. No one should bother us there." He came around the counter and started walking.

They followed him into the studio and he shut the door. The room echoed as they settled the chairs into a circle and sat down. Carly sat stiffly upright and turned her body away from Destiny. Destiny leaned back and covered her head with her hood. Her chin was tucked to her chest and her hands were deep in her pocket.

Susan sat next to her and leaned forward. "Destiny has told me her side, and Carly has told you her side. I would like to know what was said to you and I'm sure you would like to know what was said to me," Susan said gesturing with her hands. "This was a very emotional experience for both of the girls. I want to make sure that we hear both sides."

Mr. Garcia looked at his watch, leaned back and crossed his ankles. "Sounds like a plan. Destiny, why don't you start. What happened today?" He leaned forward and rested his arms on his legs. Destiny just sat there, looking at her shoes.

"See, this is what I'm talking about, Mr. Garcia. She does the same thing in class. She turns into a statue and refuses to talk," Carly burst out, waving her arms. "This is a waste of time. She'll never say anything to you." Carly stood up and started pacing behind her chair.

Mr. Garcia waved a hand. "Just give her a minute," he said. Carly rolled her eyes. Turning back to Destiny, he started again. "Do you like dance class, Destiny?" She shook her head.

"Why not?"

No answer. The only sound in the room was the clock ticking.

"Is it too hard for you?"

A nod this time.

"What makes it hard for you?"

A shrug. Mr. Garcia's chair creaked as he shifted around.

Susan prompted, "Tell him what you told me."

"I don't know what she's talking about," Destiny said, still looking at the floor. "I don't know what a perrywet is, or second position, or any of it. I've never done this before and the other girls would laugh at me if I tried." Susan patted Destiny's knee.

"Now we're getting somewhere," Mr. Garcia said, rubbing his hands together. He turned to Carly. "Did you know that this was Destiny's first dance class?" Carly's face turned red and she shook her head. "I'd get upset, too, if I was asked to do things when I had no idea how to do them," Mr. Garcia went on. "It's no fun when people tease you for that."

Carly came over to Destiny's chair and knelt in front of her. There were tears in her eyes. "Oh, Destiny, I'm so sorry. I didn't know. I thought you didn't like me and were just being difficult. Will you please come back to class? I'll go slower and help you figure things out. I promise."

Destiny said, "Sorry I pushed you. I don't like it when people touch me." She held out her fist and Carly gently bumped it.

Chapter 16

Saturday night at the Moore house was laundry night. Susan went to Julie and Destiny's room to collect dirty clothes. Julie was playing with the dollhouse and Destiny was lying on her bed reading.

"Destiny, you've been wearing your sweatshirt every day this week. It needs to go in the laundry," Susan said.

Destiny shook her head and stuck her hands into the pocket. "No, I don't want it washed. It's fine the way it is."

Julie was trying a dress on her Barbie doll. She stopped and looked at Destiny. She wrinkled her nose and said, "It's starting to get stinky. You should let Mommy wash it."

"It will be the first load, I promise. You'll have it back in an hour, tops," Susan said, holding her hand up like she was taking an oath. She waited expectantly. Destiny shook her head again.

Susan snapped her fingers. "I've got an idea," she said. She turned and left the room. She came back quickly with a black sweatshirt. "You can wear my sweatshirt while I wash yours. Deal?"

Destiny looked at her for a long time and then slowly pulled her hands out of her pocket. She was holding her notebook and pencil. "I guess," she said.

"What's that?" Julie asked, pointing at Destiny's notebook.

Destiny quickly shoved it under her pillow. "Nothing," she said. She took off the green sweatshirt and handed it to Susan. She took the black one, pulled it over her head, grabbed her notebook and ran out of the room.

Susan followed her slowly and went downstairs to the laundry room. She put the green sweatshirt and other clothes into the washing machine and closed the lid. Then she went into the living room. Destiny was sitting on the couch with her knees up, drawing in her notebook. Susan watched her for a minute and then walked over to sit on the couch opposite of Destiny.

Destiny closed the notebook and shoved it behind the couch cushion.

Susan said, "That notebook seems pretty important to you. You never let it out of your sight."

Destiny pulled it back out and rubbed her hand across the scarred cover. "I guess."

"I'd like to see it sometime if you'd let me," Susan said. Jackson whined and scratched at the kitchen door and she got up to let him out.

True to her word, she had the sweatshirt washed and dried within an hour. She took it up to Destiny's room and exchanged it for her black one. She watched as Destiny took the notebook out and started to put it in her pocket.

Destiny hesitated, then pulled it back out. "Susan?" she said.

"Yes?"

"You can look at it if you want." Destiny held the notebook out to her.

Susan sat on the edge of the bed and held the notebook gently in her hands. She looked at Destiny, who was watching her closely.

She opened the cover and gasped. "Oh, my! These are wonderful drawings!" She turned each page slowly and examined each drawing carefully. Each page held a new surprise. On one page she pointed at a picture of a woman with long hair eating an ice cream cone. "Who is this?"

Destiny said, "My mom."

"She's a beautiful woman," Susan said, tracing her finger along the line of the woman's hair.

"She used to be. I remember when I was little and we were happy," Destiny said.

Susan turned more pages. "Is this your cat?"

Destiny shook her head. "No. That's just a stray that lived in our backyard. I called him Fur Ball. I fed him sometimes."

Susan looked at more pages that showed animals and birds and one with an orchid on a windowsill. Then she turned the page and a sob caught in her throat. Destiny had drawn a picture of Susan and Julie sitting on the couch reading a book together.

When she reached the end, Susan closed the book carefully and handed it back to Destiny. "That book is very special. You are an amazing artist, Destiny. Thank you for sharing it with me."

Destiny allowed a small smile to cross her lips. She ducked her head and took the notebook from Susan.

"How about we replace dance class with an art class?" Susan asked, smiling.

Chapter 17

Over the next few weeks, Destiny began to relax. She opened up, little by little.

During soccer practice, she still refused to put on shorts, but she did chase after the ball when it came her way.

Swimming lessons were a no-go, but Darrin was able to convince her to sit on the piano bench and taught her a rocking rendition of 'Twinkle, Twinkle Little Star' that they played as a duet. Julie sang along with gusto and Susan filmed it all on her phone.

The hood of her sweatshirt stayed down most of the time. Destiny especially liked the drawing class. Susan bought some colored pencils. Destiny spent hours at the kitchen table with her notebook. She went back to many of her previous drawings and added color.

Her body began to fill out and she stopped wearing the green sweatshirt every day. The only thing that she had a hard time letting go of was hoarding food. She couldn't stop herself from taking extra from the table at mealtimes and putting it in her lap to save for later.

Susan watched her take food when she thought no one was looking and hide it under her napkin. She often found food in Destiny's pockets on laundry day, or in the drawer of her nightstand, or under her pillow. Susan decided not to say anything to Destiny about it. Instead, she came up with a different plan.

One day she knocked on Destiny and Julie's bedroom door. When they let her in, she had her hand behind her back. "I've got a surprise for you," she said.

Julie clapped her hands. "What is it? A puppy? A kitten? Oh, I hope it's a kitten!"

"No, it's not a new pet," Susan said. "Drum roll, please."

Destiny and Julie loudly patted their legs with their hands.

"Ta-Da!" Susan said, bringing her hand from behind her back. She was holding a small white basket. "I thought that I would leave this in here for you girls in case you ever get hungry between meals. That way you don't have to find me or go all the way to the kitchen for a snack. What do you think?"

The girls looked at each other and then at Susan. "Thanks, Mommy," said Julie. They jumped up and came over to inspect it.

Inside the basket were snack-sized bags of pretzels, crackers, and fruit snacks.

Destiny said, "Thanks." She ducked her head to hide a smile.

Susan put the basket on the dresser and left with a grin on her face and her fingers crossed. Then she went downstairs and put a matching basket on the coffee table in the living room. She also put a basket of fruit on the kitchen table. Every week she restocked the baskets with different snacks. It took a while, but eventually, Susan stopped finding food hidden around the house and in Destiny's pockets.

Julie pestered Destiny at every turn. "Please play Barbies with me, Destiny," she would beg. Or, "Could you play house with me?" Or, "Let's play school. I'll be the teacher."

Destiny ignored Julie for as long as she could. She would never admit it, but it did look like fun. She had never had anyone to play with, much less a room full of toys. When Julie wasn't looking, she would sometimes pick up the dolls or move the furniture in the dollhouse.

One day, when Julie said, "Destiny, come play with me," Destiny said, "OK." She figured if she did it once, maybe Julie would stop begging.

Julie looked surprised for a second and then grabbed Destiny's hand and pulled her upstairs. Destiny found herself playing assistant.

"They are going to have a party," Julie said. She handed Destiny a doll to dress. Then Destiny made suggestions about how they could arrange the dollhouse for the party. They spent the whole afternoon pretending the Barbie dolls were movie stars. Destiny became so involved that she started making silly voices for the dolls.

While things were beginning to get easier for Destiny on the home front, school was still a struggle. Susan had enrolled her in the same school as Julie. Every morning, when Susan dropped them off, Destiny would stand next to the fence with her hands in her pocket until the bell rang. Julie tried to get her to play, but Destiny refused.

When the bell rang, Destiny drug her feet and was the last one into the classroom. Her teacher, Miss Schmidt, had placed Destiny at the front of the room with a group of girls. One morning, the assignment was to work together to create a poster explaining how to solve a math problem in multiple ways.

Ava, a short, wiry girl with straight red hair, took charge. "Here, Tammy, you work on this part and show the addition way. Valery, you get the multiplication way. I'll write a story problem." She turned to Destiny, who was sitting with her head down on her desk. "Destiny, you can do the subtraction way." Destiny ignored her.

Miss Schmidt came over to check on their progress. Tammy pointed at Destiny, "She won't do her part. It's not fair. We do all the work and she just sits there." The other girls nodded in agreement.

"I see. Thank you for getting your parts completed anyway." She crouched down next to Destiny's desk. "What seems to be the problem?" She spoke quietly. Destiny turned her face away from Miss Schmidt.

"Hey," Miss Schmid said. "Talk to me. I can't help you if I don't know what the problem is."

Destiny sighed. She lifted her head and looked at Miss Schmidt.

"I wanted to do the addition part, but Ava told me I had to do the subtraction part. She didn't even ask. She never listens to anything I say, so I'm just not going to do it."

Miss Schmidt raised her eyebrows in surprise. This was the most that Destiny had ever said to her. She looked at the group, who had stopped working and were staring at Destiny. "Did you girls decide this together? Is Destiny right?"

Ava blushed. "I guess I did just tell her what to do."

Miss Schmidt shook her head. "I'm disappointed. How are you girls going to figure this out so that everyone has a voice in the decision?"

The group began talking and sharing ideas. When Miss Schmidt walked away to check on other groups, Destiny was working on her part of the poster, even if she wasn't talking to the rest of the group. Bad habits were hard to break and Destiny struggled to keep up with the class.

Miss Schmidt called Susan at home after school and talked to her about what had happened. "She was at least voicing her concerns," Miss Schmidt said. "It's a step in the right direction. I think that she is still struggling with asking for help when she doesn't understand and we are heading into some difficult topics. Math is definitely not Destiny's favorite subject." When she hung up, Susan called for Destiny. "Come down here for a minute, please."

"Your teacher just called and told me that she is worried about you," Susan said, wiping the table. "She says you are trying, but it seems that the work is hard. What do you think?"

Destiny shrugged her shoulders and traced a design with her finger on the table.

Susan said, "Which is harder, math or reading?"

"Math," Destiny said. She looked into the back yard and watched Jackson chasing his tail.

"Do you like reading?" Susan rinsed a glass and put it in the dishwasher.

"Sometimes." Destiny took an apple from the bowl and bit into it.

Susan snapped her fingers. "I know what we'll do. We'll get a tutor to come to the house and help you!"

Destiny didn't like that idea at all. "I don't want a tutor." She sat down and put her head on her arms.

"Not a choice," Susan said, firmly. "You are a bright young girl. You just need someone to show you how to do things in a way that makes sense to you." She wiped her hands on a towel.

Destiny looked up and wrinkled her nose. "You can't make me work with a tutor."

Susan didn't respond. She knew better than to get into a battle of words. She simply grabbed her laptop and started looking for a tutor. Destiny watched her and glared.

The next night after supper, the doorbell rang. Susan opened the door. A young woman was standing there with a black backpack slung over her shoulder. "Hi, I'm Dahlia, the tutor," she said. She had long dark hair pulled into a ponytail and deep brown eyes. She was a college student at the university, studying to be a teacher. Susan showed her to the kitchen and went to get Destiny.

Susan walked upstairs and looked in Julie and Destiny's bedroom. Julie was putting the dolls to bed. "Where's Destiny?" Susan asked.

Julie shrugged. "I don't know."

Susan looked in every room of the house, but Destiny had disappeared. She came back to the table and said, "I'm sorry. Destiny seems to be missing. Why don't you help Julie with her reading?" She called Julie down and introduced her to Dahlia.

Soon, Julie and Dahlia were giggling and having fun with the reading game that Dahlia had brought with her. Susan sat in the living room reading a book and watching the girls. Out of the corner of her eye, she watched the pantry door open a crack. She saw Destiny peek out.

80

Susan covered her smile with the book and kept watching. After about 5 minutes, the door opened all the way and Destiny walked over to the table.

Julie looked up and said, "Destiny! This is Dahlia. She came to play games with us. Want to play? This game is tons of fun. I've won three times already." She moved over and showed Destiny how to play.

Destiny sat at the table and watched for a while. When Dahlia handed her the dice, she silently rolled them. Soon, she was engrossed in the game. The three girls spent the rest of the hour playing together. When it was time for Dahlia to leave, Destiny said, "Sorry I hid from you."

Dahlia zipped up her backpack and said, "That's OK. My little brother is super shy, too. It takes time to get to know people. I'm glad you finally did come out, though. I'll see you next time." The girls went with her to the door and watched as she walked down the porch steps, then turned and waved. Destiny and Julie waved back.

Chapter 18

About a month later, Destiny and Julie were waiting outside of the school for Susan to pick them up. Cars came and picked up kids. They waited some more. Julie looked at Destiny. "Where's Mommy? Why isn't she here, yet?"

Destiny shrugged and watched the street. She was getting a bad feeling in the pit of her stomach. Susan was never late picking them up. The teacher on pick-up duty turned to them. "You are the last ones here. If your mom doesn't come in the next couple of minutes, we'll go to the office and call."

Just as they started to walk to the building, the now familiar blue minivan turned the corner and came up the street. When it pulled up to the curb, an older man with white hair stepped out of the driver's seat. Destiny took a step back. Julie, however, squealed and ran around the car, screaming, "Grandpa!" Destiny watched awkwardly while the two hugged each other. She wasn't sure what she should do.

The man straightened and looked at Destiny. "You must be Destiny," he said, holding out his one free hand. The other one was wrapped around Julie's jumping shoulders. Destiny waved awkwardly. Now she recognized him from the pictures on the mantle in the living room. "I've heard so much about you from Susan. It's nice to finally meet you. I'm Susan's dad, Grandpa Ben. Sorry I'm late. I got lost."

"Where's Mommy?" Julie asked, buckling into her car seat.

Grandpa Ben said, "She called and asked if Grandma Lucy and I would come and stay for a few days. She's not feeling well and could use some extra hands."

When they arrived at the house, they found Susan lying on one of the couches in the living room. She had a blanket wrapped around her and her eyes were closed. There were dark circles under her eyes and her skin was the color of a sheet of paper.

"Mommy?" Julie dropped her backpack by the door and ran to the couch.

Susan opened her eyes and smiled. "Hi, baby. How was your day at school?" She coughed and closed her eyes. She reached one arm out from under the blanket and gave her a hug.

Destiny stood quietly in the doorway and watched. She felt like an intruder. She felt a hand on her shoulder and jumped. Turning, she saw an older woman with short blonde hair and round glasses. "Oh, my! I didn't mean to scare you. I'm Grandma Lucy. You must be Destiny. Susan talks about you all the time."

Destiny ducked her head. "Nice to meet you."

The next day was Saturday. Susan stayed in bed, so Grandpa Ben took charge of the kids.

Over a hearty breakfast of omelets and bagels, he asked, "Who's up for doing a project?" He loved to work with his hands and was always looking for new projects.

Julie and Derrick both raised their hands. Destiny watched quietly. "Everybody to the van," he announced, waving his fork in the air.

Derrick asked, "Where are we going?"

"To the wood store," Grandpa Ben said. "I noticed some chickadees in the backyard that could use a home. We're going to build them some."

They piled into the van and drove to the home improvement store. Destiny had never been inside a building so big. It smelled like freshly cut wood. There were shelves and shelves of wood and other supplies.

Grandpa grabbed an oversized cart and led the way. They walked up and down the aisles. Grandpa pointed out supplies they needed and Julie and Derrick loaded the cart.

Destiny trailed behind. By the time they left, they had filled the shopping cart with enough wood to make an entire village for the birds.

Back at the house, Grandpa Ben pulled some equipment out of his truck. He set up saw horses and tables. He had a portable electric saw and other tools, too. He handed out safety glasses to everyone. They put them on and giggled about how they looked.

Grandpa showed them how to measure the pieces and he cut the boards to the right lengths. The drill was heavy, so Grandpa Ben wrapped his big, rough hands around their small ones to hold it straight when they drilled the holes. They glued and nailed the walls and roof and floor together. He showed them how to hold the nails and tap them into place so that they wouldn't hurt themselves. As they worked, Destiny slowly warmed up to Grandpa Ben. She watched him carefully and followed his directions. He let her take her time and didn't hover over her project.

By the time Grandma Lucy called them in for lunch, there were three houses lined up on the table, just waiting for sanding and painting.

After they ate, the kids were anxious to return to their projects. Julie wanted to paint her birdhouse bright pink with white flowers on it. Derrick painted his camouflage. Destiny decided to make hers look like the gingerbread house from Hansel and Gretel. The afternoon flew by and by dinner time they had their houses finished.

They left the birdhouses in the garage overnight to dry. On Sunday, they helped Grandpa Ben place them in a row on the fence in the back yard. He put Destiny's in the middle. "These are the best birdhouses I've ever seen," he bragged. "Those birds should pay rent to live in them. All the other birds will surely be jealous."

Susan and Grandma Lucy made a brief appearance in the back yard to see the birdhouses. Susan hugged each of them and exclaimed over their work. "I love what you have done!" she said. "Now we can watch from the kitchen and see who moves in."

Julie and Derrick beamed with pride. Destiny smiled a little and hid her face. She had never built anything like this before. She secretly thought hers was the best of the three.

The next week, Grandpa Ben and Grandma Lucy stayed at the house and took care of everything and everyone. Susan spent more and more time in bed. She seemed to be getting worse instead of better. She coughed all the time and never had any energy to do the things she used to. Some days she didn't make it out of bed at all.

The kids began a new ritual at night. They would climb onto Susan's bed and she would read them a bedtime story before hugging and kissing them good night. Even teenaged Derrick joined them. When Destiny got her hug from Susan, she could feel Susan's ribs.

On Friday, when Grandpa Ben picked them up, he was quiet. He smiled at them, but the twinkle in his eyes was gone. Usually, he sang or told jokes on the way home. Julie and Destiny picked up on his mood and stayed quiet, too. They could tell something wasn't right. The first thing Destiny noticed when they pulled into the driveway was a red SUV parked on the street in front of the house. Her stomach did a flipflop and her heart landed in her throat.

When they walked into the house, Susan, Grandma Lucy, and Laura were sitting in the living room. Their eyes were red and puffy and they were wiping tears from their faces.

Julie ran to her mother and hugged her. "Mommy, what's wrong?" she asked.

Susan hugged her and motioned to Derrick and Destiny. "Come sit down, kids. I have something to tell you."

Derrick crossed the room quickly and sat next to his mom. Destiny stood in the doorway and shook her head. Her face was white. Her eyes flitted from face to face. Her heart started to race. She wanted to run, but her feet seemed glued to the floor.

Susan took in a shaky breath and said, "There's no easy way to say this, so I'm just going to say it. I have cancer. I am going to have to have lots of treatments and it won't be easy. We are going to have to sell the house and move in with Grandpa Ben and Grandma Lucy for a while." Tears started streaming down her face. Julie buried her face in her mother's neck. Derrick put his arms around her. They both started crying.

"Are you going to die?" Julie asked, sobbing.

"Not if I can help it," her mother said, gently. She sat Julie on her lap and put her other arm around Derrick. "Come here, Destiny." Destiny walked woodenly across the room and sat stiffly by her side.

"Because we have to move, and because I'm so sick, the Social Services people won't let you come with us, Destiny," Susan said, holding her hand. "I'm so sorry." Her voice caught in her throat. "I told them you were a part of our family now and that we wanted you to stay with us, but they are going to find you a new family to live with." Julie started bawling again, Susan was crying, the whole room was awash in tears.

Destiny sat, as still as stone. It felt as if someone had punched her in the stomach and knocked all the wind out of her. Panic overcame her and she ran upstairs to her room. She stumbled on a doll that Julie had left in the middle of the floor. Jerking open a dresser drawer, she pulled out her green sweatshirt and put it on.

Chapter 19

Destiny reached under her bed and grabbed the red suitcase. She took her clothes out of the dresser and shoved them inside. She picked up her notebook, pencil and colored pencils off the bedside table and put them into her oversized pocket.

Taking one more look around the pink and white room, she walked out. She didn't know where she was going, but she knew that she wasn't a part of the family anymore. Destiny didn't want to go to a new house. She didn't want to meet a new family, share a room with a new little girl. She had started to think of these people as her family, but now she realized that she was a nobody. An extra. A burden to pass around when they didn't want her anymore.

Tiptoeing down the stairs, she made it to the front door and outside. She ran down the sidewalk and through the neighborhood. The suitcase banged and bounced on the rough sidewalk behind her. At the end of the street, she came to the park where she and Julie and Derrick went to play frequently. The climbing structure had a little plastic fort perched on top. Destiny climbed up inside and sat there. She wrapped her arms around herself and rocked back and forth as silent tears streamed down her face. She didn't know what to do. She didn't have a plan.

Hearing someone call her name, Destiny shrank as small as she could. She held her breath and hoped that she wouldn't be found. Several more voices called out for her. She recognized Grandpa Ben's deep voice, and

Derrick's cracking one. Laura's voice joined them. They were coming closer. Then she heard someone climbing up the ladder to her hideout. Derrick's face appeared in the opening.

Turning his head, he yelled, "I found her! Grandpa! She's in here!"

"Go away," Destiny hissed. "Leave me alone!" She tried to kick him, but he was too far away.

Derrick's head disappeared as he climbed back down. Another head appeared. It was Laura. She took one look at Destiny, then backed away. "I'll take it from here. You two go back to the house and let everyone know she's OK." She waited until Derrick and Grandpa Ben left, then climbed into the tiny space and curled up across from Destiny.

Laura didn't say anything, just sat there. She could feel the hurt coming off the little girl like steam. She looked at the red suitcase, the green sweatshirt, the tear-streaked face. There were no words to say that would take away the sting of what Destiny felt. Tears pricked Laura's eyes, too, as she looked at this beautiful child, whose world had just crumbled, yet again. Who was trying to hold herself together when she desperately needed someone who would love her unconditionally, hold her, protect her from bad things, belong to her.

They sat in the fort for a very long time. Destiny cried herself out. She felt alone, so very alone. Laura felt like a failure. The air inside that little space was thick with dark thoughts. It was after dark before the two emerged from the hiding spot. It took a lot of convincing to get Destiny to come out.

Laura had found another family for her to stay with. They had five foster children already, all teenage boys, and were not well equipped to deal with a headstrong little girl. Destiny only lasted two days with them.

Over the course of the next month, Destiny moved five times to five different foster families. Each one with their own issues. Each one willing to try, but ultimately giving up on her.

The more homes she moved to, the more belligerent Destiny became. She was also becoming aggressive. In one home, she pulled pictures off walls and smashed a brand new 72-inch television. In another home, she spit on the foster mother and pulled her hair. It didn't take much to set her off. She wanted to be left alone and would lash out when she wasn't.

Destiny also had the opposite extreme. She would sit for hours in a corner with her knees pulled up. She would stare through people when they spoke to her. She refused to take a shower or wash her clothes. The dark green sweatshirt never came off. The only time she was active was when she was drawing in her notebook. The pages became filled with images from Susan's house. The dog, Jackson, chasing a ball. Julie and her dollhouse. Derrick playing football. The family sitting at the dinner table laughing. Grandma Lucy baking cookies. Grandpa Ben and his saw.

Every time Laura came to check on her, the worry lines in her forehead deepened. One day, Laura found her huddled in a closet, in the dark, smelling of old sweat and urine.

"Destiny?" Laura said, opening the door. "What's this? Why are you in here?"

No response. Destiny had her head on her knees.

Laura slid down to the floor next to her. "Sweetie, please look at me." Destiny stiffened as Laura put a hand on her knee.

"I can tell that you are unhappy here," Laura said. "I know you miss Susan and Julie and Derrick and the others. I'm sorry you couldn't stay with them." Destiny scooted as far away from Laura as she could in the small space. Laura sighed and dropped her hand to her lap. "Let's go back to my office and see if I can find you a better place to stay, OK?"

Destiny scrambled to her feet, pushed past Laura and ran to the car. She stood by the door pulling on the handle until Laura unlocked it. Then she flung it open and climbed in. Laura put her suitcase in the back and went around to the driver's side.

As they drove, Laura gripped the steering wheel hard. Her stomach was in knots and there were tears in her eyes. She knew what kids like Destiny turned into. She knew they built huge walls around their hearts. She could already see it happening. She clenched her jaw, determined to find a way to help Destiny.

Her stomach growled suddenly. Looking at her watch, she realized that it was later than she thought. Both she and Destiny had missed their dinner. Glancing over at Destiny, she said, "Are you hungry? I'm starving."

Destiny gave a small nod, staring out the window.

Seeing a popular Mexican restaurant, Laura pulled into the parking lot. The outside was covered in yellow stucco and had arched windows all along the front. Inside, the floor was red tile and the walls were covered in murals. There was soft guitar music playing in the background. The waitress, wearing a red, white, and green dress with a black apron, seated them in a booth that had ornate carvings above the headrests painted in bright colors. She placed a basket of corn chips and a small dish of salsa in the center of the table.

Destiny had never been to a restaurant like this one. The only Mexican food she ever had come from a fast food place. She turned in her seat so she could see everything.

Laura ordered tacos for both of them. When the food arrived, Destiny started picking up the food and shoving it in her mouth like she hadn't eaten in a month.

"Hey! Slow down," Laura said. "You'll choke if you don't chew your food."

Destiny smiled a small smile and chewed. She had never tasted anything like it. It was warm and cheesy and spicy.

Laura watched her and smiled. There was the little girl she knew was in there. If only there was a way to bring her out more.

As they were finishing their meal, Destiny started squirming and said, "I need to use the bathroom."

Laura stood up. "Come on. I'll show you where it is." They walked toward the far wall. There was a young couple sitting in a booth on their way and Laura glanced at them, then stopped and laughed.

"Jake? Chrissy?" Laura said. "It's so good to see you!"

The couple stood up and hugged Laura. "Laura! It's been too long! How have you been?"

Laura felt a tug on her sleeve. She looked down and Destiny said, "I really need to use the bathroom."

Excusing herself, she took Destiny down the hallway and waited for her by the sinks. When they came out, they stopped by Jake and Chrissy's table.

"Sorry about that. You can't ignore the call of nature," Laura said, laughing. "Destiny, this is Jake and Chrissy Preston. They are friends of mine. They also used to be my neighbors. Jake, Chrissy, meet Destiny."

Destiny gave a small wave and then put her hands into her pocket and looked at the floor.

Chrissy said, "Nice to meet you, Destiny."

Laura said, "What brings you here tonight? You are both dressed up so nicely. Date night?"

"We are actually celebrating something special tonight," Chrissy said. She smiled proudly. "We just finished the last step to become foster parents! All our home visits are done, all the paperwork is in. Now we are just waiting to be put on the list."

Laura's jaw dropped. "You've got to be kidding! That's wonderful news! Congratulations!" She couldn't believe her ears. This couldn't be happening right now, right here. This was the perfect couple for Destiny. They were young energetic people with the right personality and temperament.

She reached into her purse and pulled out a business card. She handed it to Chrissy and said, "Could you come over to my office when you finish your meal. I might have something you can help me with, but I'd rather not talk about it here." After she gave them each a hug, she paid the waitress and took Destiny out to the car.

"Destiny, we are going to go to my office for a while. I need to make a phone call and then Jake and Chrissy are going to come and visit us, OK?" She smiled at Destiny.

"Am I going to have to go home with them?" Destiny said. There was dread in her voice.

Laura nodded. "Maybe."

At the office, Destiny sat on the couch in the waiting area and drew in her notebook while Laura went to her desk. She pulled up the Preston's file on her computer and confirmed that they were indeed qualified to take Destiny into their home. Relief washed over her. One obstacle remained. Would they be willing to take on this challenging child? Would it be a good fit, or would Destiny once again end up in her office, rejected, with her heart stomped on?

An hour later, Laura's cell phone rang. She went downstairs to unlock the door for Jake and Chrissy. It was very dark outside and the air had grown cold enough to show their breath.

"We didn't know that you worked for Social Services," Jake said. "That's uncanny!"

Laura laughed. "You have no idea how grateful I am that I bumped into the two of you tonight."

Laura led the way to the elevator and explained Destiny's situation as they walked. She wanted them to know exactly what they were getting into. She told them about Destiny's behavior, about how easily she shut down when faced with adversity or rejection.

"You've got to understand where she's coming from," Laura said. "She's had a lot of trauma in her young life. She's been neglected, abused, abandoned, rejected. More than anything, she needs to feel protected. Once you've cleared that hurdle, then you can work on connecting with her. She won't trust you unless she feels safe with you."

Chrissy grabbed Jake's hand. They looked at each other and nodded. Turning to Laura, with tears in her eyes, Chrissy said, "We'd love to have Destiny in our home. I had a miscarriage a year ago and found out that I won't ever be able to have children. We still want a family, though. I know it sounds cliché, but we really want to make a difference in the life of a child that desperately needs love."

Chapter 20

The first few days were rough on everyone. Destiny stayed in her shell and hid most of the time in the bedroom that the Prestons had prepared for her. She only came out of her room to eat her meals, which she did quickly. She never spoke to either Jake or Chrissy. After she was done, she returned to her room and shut the door.

Chrissy would stand at the door and listen, but she never heard a sound. It was as if Destiny was a ghost. Chrissy paced in the hall outside Destiny's room and chewed her nails to the quick.

Jake said, "Remember what Laura told us, give her time. She's been through a lot. She has to learn to trust us. She's given her heart away twice and had it ripped to shreds, first, by her own mother, and then by her last foster family."

Chrissy nodded. "I know, I know. It's just so hard, you know? There's got to be something we can do to help her feel more at home."

Jake wrapped his arms around her and pulled her to him. He stroked her long, blonde hair and said, "I love you so much. You are so sensitive and caring. Be patient. She'll come around."

"I hope you are right, Jake," Chrissy said, sighing. She closed her eyes and listened to the steady beat of Jake's heart.

Jake and Chrissy tried to get Destiny to talk to them, but never pushed her, never forced her to participate, just accepted her and did everything they could to let her know that they cared for her. After what Laura had told them, they knew that they might be in for a long wait.

One night, long after they had gone to bed, Chrissy woke with a start.

"Jake, wake up!" she whispered, shaking his shoulder. "There's someone downstairs."

Jake sat up and listened. The floor in the dining room creaked. Hinges of a door protested as it was opened slowly. Chrissy covered her mouth. Jake slid out of bed. "You stay here. I'll go check it out," he whispered.

He crept out of the room and padded softly down the stairs. Chrissy followed him. She stopped at the top of the stairs.

A soft light shown from under the kitchen pantry door. Jake made his way slowly across the floor, stepping over the creaky spots. He reached out and grasped the doorknob. Taking a deep breath, he threw it open. It took a second for his eyes to adjust to the light. There, sitting on the floor, was Destiny, her mouth full of cookies.

For a second, she froze, her eyes big, her cheeks bulging. Then she scrambled to her feet and tried to run past Jake. His broad shoulders filled the doorway and gave her no room to escape. She tried to squeeze past, but he refused to move. She tried to yell at him, but her mouth was too full of cookies. She head-butted his stomach and kicked his shins. All to no avail.

"Hey! Fancy meeting you here," he said, laughing. "Either you are an awfully big raccoon or a hungry young lady with a sweet tooth." He took one of the cookies that Destiny was still holding and popped it into his mouth. "You are doing this all wrong," he said. "Come on, I'll show you."

Destiny eyed him suspiciously. She backed up and watched him. Jake picked up the package of cookies and went into the kitchen. He put the cookies on the table, went to the fridge and grabbed a jug of milk. He filled two glasses and set them on the table. He sat in a chair and patted the one next to it. "Come here, Destiny. I'll teach you the right way to eat these."

Destiny took a step closer. Jake picked up a cookie, twisted the two halves apart, and licked out the cream filling. Then he dunked the chocolate parts in the milk and chewed them up. Turning to look at Destiny standing in the doorway of the pantry, he said, "Care to try one?"

Destiny walked over to the table and climbed onto the chair. Jake handed her a cookie and they both twisted, licked, and dunked. Destiny smiled at Jake and Jake laughed.

Chrissy came into the kitchen. "What's going on here?"

"We are having a lesson on the proper way to eat cookies in the middle of the night," Jake said. He held out a cookie. "Care to join us?"

Chrissy pulled up a chair and Jake poured her a glass of milk. Destiny shyly handed her a cookie. Between the three of them, they polished off the whole package of cookies.

Chapter 21

The next morning, Chrissy went into Destiny's room. Gently, she shook Destiny's shoulder. "Time to wake up, sleepyhead." Destiny sat up quickly and rubbed her eyes. She pushed her tousled brown hair away from her face. She stared at Chrissy for a long minute. Her eyes roamed around the room, looking at the plain grey curtains, the cream-colored walls, the simple dresser. Taking a deep breath, she asked, "Am I going back to Laura's office?" She pulled her knees up to her chest and wrapped her arms around them.

Chrissy sat on the side of the bed. Shaking her blonde ponytail, she said, "Nope. You are going to go to work with us. Let's get dressed and eat some breakfast. After we stop by the Center, we are going to go shopping and get you some things for your room. Do you want to pick out your sheets and blankets and pillows? The stuff I have in here isn't much suited for a little girl."

"But I messed up. I'm not going to be here long enough for it to matter," Destiny said. She looked down at her fingernails. There were cookie crumbs around them.

Chrissy frowned. "What do you mean?"

"You seem like a nice enough lady, but last night I broke into your closet thing and ate all your cookies. I do bad stuff all the time. I can't be trusted. Once you get to know me you won't want me to stay with you anymore. Nobody does. This is the eighth house I've been to." Destiny

97

pushed the covers back, stood up and walked out into the hall. She went into the bathroom and gently closed the door.

Chrissy sat still on the edge of the bed. Her heart was breaking for this young girl. A lump formed in her throat and she fought back tears. Laura had warned them that Destiny had been through a lot and put up some pretty big walls. She was shocked at how calmly Destiny spoke about her situation. Like it was normal not to be wanted, or loved. Chrissy straightened her shoulders and stood up. She was determined to not let Destiny's negativity affect her. Somehow, someway, she would break through those walls and reach the hurting child inside that tough shell.

She went downstairs to find Jake. He was sitting at the table, reading some papers. Looking up, he asked, "How's our little present this morning?" He took a bite of toast.

"She's OK. A little scared still. Putting up a prickly attitude. She wanted to know if we were taking her back to Laura's office because of last night. Poor thing. At least she's started talking."

When Destiny came downstairs to the kitchen, she was wearing her jeans and her dark green sweatshirt. She stopped and stood in the doorway, hands in pocket, rubbing her pencil, not sure what to say or do. Jake pulled out the chair next to him and patted the seat with his hand. "Hop up here, Destiny. Let's get you some cereal." She walked around the table and pulled out a different chair, far away from him.

Chrissy and Jake raised their eyebrows at each other. Then Chrissy slid a bowl to Destiny. "We have corn flakes or raisin bran if you want cereal. Or you could have toast and peanut butter like Jake." Destiny filled her bowl with corn flakes and carefully added milk. She ate quickly and drank the juice Jake poured for her. Never once did she look up at either of them.

Chrissy cleared her throat and tried again. "I was going to replace those boring old curtains and bedspread anyway. You can help me pick out new ones, can't you?

Destiny shrugged. It didn't matter to her, but they were pretty ugly. "Do they have to be pink? One of the rooms I stayed in was all pink. I really don't like pink too much."

Chrissy smiled. "Want to know a secret? I don't like pink either. We'll pick out something together."

Soon after, they all piled into Jake's big, dirty black Suburban and headed out. After about ten minutes of driving, he turned into a parking lot, crunched through the gravel and stopped in front of a single-story blue metal building. It had a large white garage door on the left end. On the right was a glass door.

Destiny climbed out of the back seat and looked around. Across the busy road were railroad tracks. A big field stretched out beside the building and brown weed stalks stuck up everywhere. It reminded her a little of the area around the big ditch by her mom's house.

There was a wooden sign on a post stuck in a small patch of grass by the glass door. It had white lettering on it. Destiny couldn't make out the words from where she was standing.

Jake came around the Suburban and spread his arms wide. "Welcome to the Raptor Rehabilitation Center," he said, puffing out his chest. He smiled at Destiny and waited for her reaction.

She rolled her eyes at him and stuck her hands into her pocket.

Jake chuckled and said, "You are in for a treat. You've never seen anything like this, I guarantee! Come inside and I'll show you."

Chrissy put her arm around Destiny's shoulders and squeezed. "Don't mind him. He's just a little proud of this place. He helped design and build it. I hope his head will fit through the door."

Destiny stepped away from Chrissy and followed Jake to the glass door. He unlocked the door and held it open for Chrissy and Destiny.

Destiny walked into what looked to be a store. There was a cash register on a counter on one side of the room. Stuffed animals filled a bin and jewelry hung on racks on the wall. A shelf, full of books, filled another wall. At the back of the room, just past the cash register, was another door. They walked through it and down a short hallway.

Jake flipped some light switches. They were standing in a huge warehouse space. It was cluttered with equipment, tables, and boxes. He led them to another door in the back wall. When he opened it, they walked outside again under a large roof. They walked between wooden crates stacked two high. When they reached the end of the crates, there were large wooden enclosures on each side of a walkway that reached two stories tall. Destiny walked up next to the nearest one. The walls were made of slats. She put her eye to a gap and peered inside. Destiny could see tree branches and boxes. And birds. Big birds. Beautiful birds. Staring back at her was an owl. It was golden brown with specks of black on its feathers. Its eyes were very large and yellow. It tilted its head as it stared back at Destiny, whose mouth was open in a small 'o'.

"Whoa," she said, taking a step back. "It's a real owl!" She couldn't help herself. She had never seen anything like this before. She walked down the aisle and stopped at every enclosure. She studied each bird in turn. Some birds were huge and others were as small as her head. She recognized some of them, but others she had never seen before. Reaching the end of the row, she turned around and walked slowly back. "What is this place?" she asked, in awe. Jake and Chrissy had been watching her, enjoying her reaction. Jake had his hands tucked into the front pockets of his jeans. He rocked back on his heels and smiled.

Chrissy said, "These are all raptors, sometimes called birds of prey. They are here because they are either sick or injured. Our job is to fix them up, get them well, and if they can hunt for themselves, send them back to the wild where they came from."

Destiny forgot that she was supposed to be bored. "What happens to the ones that can't hunt for themselves," she asked.

"Some of those birds become permanent members of our family here at the Center if they have the right temperament and prove that they can tolerate being around humans. They stay here for the rest of their lives and help us teach people about raptors and how important they are to our environment. They go to schools, libraries, anywhere we can go to talk to people," Jake said. He went over and stood next to Destiny. "What do you think? Pretty cool, huh?"

Destiny slipped back behind her protective shield. "I don't know. I guess." She kept her face emotionless and shrugged her shoulders.

"Today we are just here to do some feeding and check on a few that we bandaged up this week. We'll be out of here in no time." Chrissy led the way back inside.

"What do you feed them?" Destiny asked.

"We try to feed them the same food that they would eat in the wild. We want to give them every chance at survival in the wild. Most of them eat small mammals, like rabbits, rats, and mice," Jake explained. They went into a small room that looked like a kitchen, with countertops and freezers, but no stove.

"Mice and rats? Are they alive?" Destiny wrinkled her nose and shuddered.

Chrissy laughed. "We only use live ones when we are doing hunting training before we release a bird into the wild. The rest get frozen ones that we get delivered and keep in the freezer."

The Prestons came out of the food prep area with large white tubs. They carried large silver instruments that they used to place food in each enclosure. Destiny watched as they stopped at each enclosure to deliver breakfast.

Destiny's hands were back in her pocket. She itched to pull out her notebook and sketch some of these animals, but she decided against it. She made mental notes that she could turn into drawings when she was alone in her room.

Chapter 22

Destiny missed Susan and Julie and Jackson the dog and Derrick, even though he could be annoying at times. She thought of them every day and wanted so badly to go back to their house. She wondered if Susan was feeling better, or if she had gotten sicker. She wondered what it was like at Grandpa Ben's house. She wondered if they missed her, or if they wanted her back. She spent a lot of time looking at the pictures she had drawn of them in her notebook.

Jake and Chrissy enrolled Destiny in a nearby school. This one was bigger than the one she had gone to with Julie. There were lots of hallways and lots of students. The office was a hive of activity and Destiny grew more and more nervous, the longer they sat waiting and filling out paperwork. She started bouncing her knee up and down. She tucked her hands into the pocket of her green sweatshirt and rubbed her pencil. Her eyes darted around the room.

An older woman wearing a blue dress and sensible shoes came out of an inner room. She walked up to Jake and Chrissy. "Hello. My name is Mrs. Simpson. I'm the principal here at Lander Elementary." She held out her hand to Jake and then Chrissy. They introduced themselves and then introduced Destiny.

"We've been expecting you," Mrs. Simpson said. She smiled at Destiny. "Welcome to Lander. I'm sure you will fit right in. Shall we show you to your new classroom?"

Jake and Chrissy stood up. Chrissy pulled Destiny up by the elbow when Destiny didn't move. They followed after Mrs. Simpson as she made her way through a confusing maze of hallways and stairs. Destiny tuned out the tour guide routine and watched her feet. "You'll get used to it, Destiny. For the first few days, we'll make sure you have a buddy to show you around."

After what seemed like forever, they stopped at a closed door that was covered in paper frogs. Each one had a name on it. The frogs had obviously been colored and cut out by the students as some were rainbow striped, some had spots, and some were not colored at all. Mrs. Simpson knocked on the door. A student opened the door.

"Will you tell Mr. Petra to come here, please," Mrs. Simpson said. A few seconds later a tall man wearing a black button-down shirt and gray slacks filled the doorway.

Mrs. Simpson smiled her toothy smile and said, "Mr. Petra, here is your new student, Destiny. These are her guardians, Jake and Chrissy Preston."

Mr. Petra looked down at Destiny. He sort of smiled, without showing his teeth. "Welcome to the 5th grade, Destiny. Come in and get settled. Nice to meet you," he said to Jake and Chrissy. His voice was deep. Mr. Petra dipped his head and stepped to the side to allow Destiny to enter.

"Bye, Destiny. We'll pick you up out front after school," Chrissy said as the door closed.

Destiny stood by the door and assessed the room. It was messy and crowded. Instead of desks, there were rectangular tables with chairs on all sides. There were students everywhere. Some were sitting on exercise balls, some were standing at tables that had been raised to counter height, some were sitting on the floor. It was also very noisy. Destiny could feel her heart start to beat faster.

"Come with me," Mr. Petra said. He walked through the maze to the front of the room. Lifting a chair from a corner, he set it at an empty spot at a table. "You can park yourself here for now. I move kids around a lot, so don't get used to it." Then he walked away, leaving Destiny standing there, staring after him.

Destiny, not knowing what else to do, put her new backpack on the back of the chair and sat down. She watched the students around her as they worked on a poster of some kind. No one spoke to her or looked at her.

Suddenly, a bell rang on the teacher's desk. "Everyone, stop working and turn in your posters. We'll get back to them tomorrow. Look at the board to see what station you will be working at for math today. Oh, and say hi to.... what's your name again?" Everyone turned to look at Destiny.

Her face turned red. "Destiny," she mumbled.

"Speak up," Mr. Petra said, "No one can hear a mumbler."

Destiny felt more heat flush into her cheeks. "My name is Destiny," she said louder.

Turning to the class, Mr. Petra said, "Everyone has 30 seconds to get to your spots, starting now." Mr. Petra began counting backward while at the same time walking to the front of the room. The students scrambled to get in place before he was finished.

"Aaaannnnndddd, zero," said Mr. Petra. He dropped a paper and pencil on the table in front of Destiny. "See what you can do with this," he said, not even looking at Destiny.

For a moment, Destiny just sat there, staring at Mr. Petra's tall back. She glanced at the paper. It was covered in large numbers. To Destiny, it felt like there were at least a hundred problems.

Suddenly, it felt like the room was crushing her. It was hard to breathe. She pulled her hood over her head and put her face against the cool table. Closing her eyes, she tried to block out everything around her. Out of nowhere, her hood was yanked off her head.

"We don't wear hats or hoods in this building," came Mr. Petra's voice behind her. "Sit up and get started." Raising his voice, he said, "Class, do we sit and do nothing in this room?"

There was a chorus of, "No, Mr. Petra."

"Of course not. Everyone has a job to do here. What is your job?"

Again, a chorus. "To learn."

"That's right!" Lowering his voice, Mr. Petra said, "What seems to be the hold-up, Andrea?"

Destiny gripped her new pencil with both hands and broke it. Clenching her teeth, she said, "My name is Destiny."

"Well, DESTINY, why aren't you working? I'm NOT giving you a new pencil, just because you broke yours," Mr. Petra said.

With her blood pulsing in her ears, Destiny picked up the math sheet and slowly crumpled it into a little ball. With all her strength, she hurled it across the room. "You and your math paper can SUCK IT!" she said.

The room grew deathly silent. Mr. Petra drew himself up to his full height. "You are here to LEARN. This is your JOB. Go pick up that paper and get to WORK." He pointed at where the paper had landed and stared down at Destiny.

"No," Destiny said, crossing her arms and putting her head down again. "Leave me alone."

"You WILL do your work. If not NOW, then at LUNCHTIME."

Destiny turned her back on Mr. Petra and said, "YOU CAN'T MAKE ME!"

Mr. Petra's face was turning bright red. His lips crushed into a tight line. The entire class held its breath. "You WILL do your work, just like everyone else in this class. Eddie," he said, snapping his fingers, "get that paper for me." The student ran over and handed the ruined paper to Mr. Petra. He flattened it and set it back down on the desk. He picked up the broken pencil and placed it in Destiny's hand.

Destiny reared up and flipped the table upside down. The students jumped at the crash. "I SAID I'M NOT DOING YOUR STUPID MATH!

JUST LEAVE ME ALONE!" Destiny pushed kids out of her way and ran out of the classroom. She ran down the hallway and around the corner. Seeing a dark, empty classroom, she went inside and hid in a corner. She pulled her hood up and wiped angry tears from her cheeks.

Ten minutes went by and the classroom lights came on. "There you are!"

Destiny looked up and saw Mrs. Simpson staring at her. She put her head back down on her knees. Mrs. Simpson walked over pulled up a chair. Destiny scooted herself around until her back was to Mrs. Simpson. Mrs. Simpson started to talk, so Destiny covered her ears with her hands. She stayed like that for a while and then looked around. Mrs. Simpson was still sitting there, arms crossed, just watching her.

Destiny rolled her eyes at the principal. "Can't you people take a hint? I don't like you; I don't like your school; I don't want to be here. Just. Leave. Me. Alone."

Mrs. Simpson was quiet for a minute. Then she said, "It doesn't work like that around here. Everyone is expected to do their job. I'm not going to argue with you, Destiny." She stood up and looked at the door. "I think the class that belongs here is coming back. I suggest we go down to my office unless you want them staring at you when they come in here."

Destiny glared at her. Then, students started coming in. Destiny stood up and walked stiffly out of the room, purposely bumping into students with her shoulder on her way out. Mrs. Simpson followed her out and placed a hand on the middle of Destiny's back. Destiny shrugged her off and said, "Quit touching me!"

"I will, as long as you stay right next to me," Mrs. Simpson said.

Destiny let out an exasperated sigh. "Fine."

They walked down the hall. Mrs. Simpson stopped in front of the door that had frogs on it. "You're crazy if you think I'm going back in there," Destiny said. She started to back away.

"You stay right there," Mrs. Simpson warned. "I'm not taking you in there, yet. I need to speak with Mr. Petra. Then we'll go down to my office and sort this out." She knocked at the door and spoke quietly with Mr. Petra. Destiny leaned against the wall and stared at her shoes.

When Mrs. Simpson turned around, she was holding the wrinkled math paper and broken pencil in her hand. She motioned for Destiny to come with her. The rest of the trip to the office was made in silence.

Mrs. Simpson opened the door to her office and went inside. She pointed to a student desk in the corner. "Have a seat, Destiny." She sat. Mrs. Simpson dragged her office chair over next to the small desk. She held the offending math assignment between her thumb and finger and waved it in the air. Destiny watched her from under hooded eyelids. Her hands were in her pocket and her thumb rubbed her red pencil furiously.

"Seems like an awfully big deal over a little old piece of paper," Mrs. Simpson commented. She put the paper on the desk and smoothed it with her hands. The diamond ring she was wearing caught the light. "Did you even look at the problems on the page before you sent it across the room?"

Destiny silently stared at her.

Mrs. Simpson turned the sheet towards herself. "Three times two. Six times zero. Seven times one. Multiplication. Do you know how to multiply?"

Destiny continued to stare at her. She clenched her fingers into fists. She clenched her jaw. Mrs. Simpson stared back. Then Mrs. Simpson sat back in her seat, laced her fingers together behind her head, and said, "I can help you with this if you want, or you can do it by yourself. Your choice. I can also sit here and keep talking to you all day long. Seems to me that you don't want that, so if you want me to be quiet, you should pick up the pencil and start doing your work. If you do that, I'll go over there to my desk and do my work. Oh, and don't worry, if you ruin that page, I'll get you another one to do." Then she smiled sweetly.

Destiny's eyes shifted from Mrs. Simpson's face to the paper and back again. She glared at Mrs. Simpson. Then she picked up the pencil. She hated this woman; she hated this school. "Fine. Whatever," she said. She looked at the math problems and started working. Mrs. Simpson slid her rolling chair across the room to her computer and started typing. She glanced over at Destiny every once in a while, to make sure she was still working, but left her alone.

Destiny looked at the paper. She didn't care about the work. She started writing random numbers under the problems and quickly finished the first row. She glanced up at Mrs. Simpson, who was watching her. Mrs. Simpson frowned and shook her head. "Do it right, or do it over. Your choice."

Rolling her eyes, she turned back to the page and started over. She worked the problems out slowly and finally finished the page. By then, Destiny's stomach was rumbling. Mrs. Simpson looked at the paper and said, "I knew you could do it. Let's go back to your classroom and give it to Mr. Petra. Then you can go get some lunch."

They made their way back through the maze of hallways to the frog covered door. Mrs. Simpson and Destiny went in, but the room was empty. Mrs. Simpson pointed to the table that was still overturned at the front of the room. "You need to clean up the mess you made, too, Destiny. Let's go turn the table over." Destiny followed her and they picked up the table and chairs that had been knocked over. While they were doing that, the classroom door opened and Mr. Petra walked in.

When Mr. Petra saw them, he frowned. Mrs. Simpson said, "I think that Destiny has something to say to you, isn't that right, Destiny?" Both adults looked at Destiny and waited.

Destiny said, "Sorry."

Mr. Petra crossed his arms and leaned forward. "For what, Destiny? It isn't an apology unless you know what you are sorry for."

"Sorry for messing up your room," Destiny mumbled, shifting her weight from foot to foot.

Mr. Petra said, "Apology accepted. I hope this is the last time we have this happen." Then he turned, walked over to his desk and sat down.

Mrs. Simpson took Destiny down to the cafeteria and showed her how to navigate the steam tables and computer system. Taking her tray, she looked around the room. Seeing an empty table by the far wall, she walked over and turned her back on the students. She put her hood up and made it clear that she didn't want any company. The other students steered clear of her. Even the adults who were monitoring the cafeteria left her alone.

Out on the playground, Destiny sat on a bench with her hands in her pockets and watched the other students play. She couldn't wait for this day to be over. When the bell rang, she slowly made her way inside and followed her class to their room. She managed to make it through the rest of the day without incident, mostly because the other students gave her a wide berth and Mr. Petra ignored her.

Back at the Preston's house that afternoon, Destiny went up to her room and curled up on her bed under the new comforter that she had picked out with Chrissy. She had chosen a light purple one that reminded her of lilacs. Chrissy and Jake's orange cat, Muffin, liked Destiny's comforter, too. It came and curled up next to Destiny and purred. Destiny stroked its fur slowly and watched Muffin's eyes close. Over and over again, she ran her hand down Muffin's back. Two tears ran down her cheeks. She didn't bother to wipe them away.

Chapter 23

Every day, either Chrissy or Jake would meet Destiny outside the school in the afternoon and take her to the Raptor Rehab Center. They started giving her small chores to do, like raking leaves. She complied, mostly because if she didn't, she would have to sit in the office with them and answer questions about her day. Besides, raking meant that she could stand outside the enclosures and watch the birds. She didn't mind doing the chores, really, but she wouldn't tell them that.

It was peaceful at the Center, but not quiet by any means. The birds screeched and called and ruffled their feathers. Destiny liked this kind of noise. It helped her think. She knew it was only a matter of time before these people sent her away. Just like everyone else had. They didn't want her either, she knew. They would get sick of her, or she'd do something they didn't like, and then get rid of her. She spent her chore time thinking about running away for real.

She had it all planned out. She would fill her red suitcase with the food that she had hidden in her dresser and just walk away. *Better that I leave, than have them kick me out,* she thought. She planned to go back to her mother's house. She thought she knew the way. Then she thought about what was waiting for her when she got there. Exactly nothing. Maybe Fur Ball would be there, but she doubted it. It had been months since she last saw him. He had probably moved on.

But somehow, there was a draw for her here. Jake and Chrissy really listened. They involved her but didn't push her. They gave her space. Then there were the birds. The more she watched them, the more she noticed things about their personalities. She noticed their moods and preferences. She couldn't wait to see them at the end of the day. Sometimes, the thought of seeing them was the only thing that helped her through the day. She would sit in class and watch the clock, willing it to move faster. She wanted to check on them and see how they were doing. Was the new little kestrel's wing healing right? Was the big barn owl tracking with his eyes? Had the turkey vulture's tail feathers started to grow out?

One of Destiny's favorite birds was a large male barn owl. His white feathers and the orange ring around his face really made him stand out among the other birds. He was calm when the other birds became frenetic. He let the vets and volunteers work around and with him without complaint.

Destiny secretly called him Grandpa. She knew that he was a wild animal and not a pet and that the staff at the Rehab Center frowned on giving names to the birds. But she couldn't help herself. He just looked and acted the way that she thought a grandpa would. He reminded her of Grandpa Ben. The bird had broken his right wing, and it had never healed properly. As a result, he held it awkwardly at his side and he couldn't fly. Even his waddling walk reminded her of Grandpa Ben.

Destiny enjoyed the birds for the fact that they didn't demand anything from her. They didn't ask her endless questions. They didn't pester her about her homework or taking showers. They didn't care if she wore her sweatshirt every day. They simply minded their own business and accepted her as she was. So, the little red suitcase remained empty under her bed.

Chapter 24

The calendar in Mr. Petra's classroom said it was December. For the first time she could remember, Destiny wasn't dreading winter break from school. She knew that she would be warm, and fed, and safe during the break. She wouldn't have to scrounge through people's garbage or beg at a restaurant for something to eat or steal from the grocery store. She wouldn't have to endure her mother's drunken boyfriends who liked to hit her. She knew that Chrissy and Jake cared about her. Life had settled into a routine. She still didn't talk much but was becoming more compliant.

One morning, as Destiny came down the stairs, she overheard Chrissy and Jake talking in the kitchen. "Destiny's only got one more week of school. What are we going to do with her during break?" Jake said.

Destiny stopped halfway down the stairs. She held her breath. This was it. Her fears were going to be realized. They were going to send her away.

Then Chrissy said, "I looked into having her go to the day camp down at the recreation center. They have swimming, and basketball, and arts and crafts."

Destiny let her breath out. They wanted her to stay. She continued down the stairs and walked into the kitchen.

"Good morning, Sunshine," Jake said. He passed her a plate of pancakes and a bottle of syrup. "We were just talking about the fun you are going to have over your break from school. How do you feel about swimming lessons?"

Destiny poured some syrup on her pancakes before she answered. "I'd rather stay and help you at the Center. I won't be any trouble, I promise!"

Chrissy said, "Oh, honey. You'd be bored being there all day. Wouldn't you rather go to the rec center and do sports and stuff?"

"I've already taken all those classes," Destiny said. "Susan made us take them after school every day. I don't like them. I'd rather spend time at the Center with the birds." She paused. "And with you," she added.

Chrissy stopped wiping the counters and looked at her. "Really? You seem like you are bored when you are there." She looked at Jake, who shrugged his shoulders and took a swig from his coffee mug. Chrissy raised her eyebrows.

"I promise to be good," Destiny said. "I'll even help clean the rat cages." She wrinkled her nose. "I'm not bored when I'm there. Really, I'm not. I just like to listen and watch the birds. They don't bug me like people do. I don't want to go to day camp." She turned pleading eyes on Jake.

Chrissy's eyes went wide. This was the most that Destiny had ever talked to them.

Jake set down his cup. "I don't see a problem with it, as long as you promise to do as you are told and help out around the Rehab Center. It's not a place for kids, you know. You can't go wandering off by yourself. The birds need lots of peace and quiet to heal. They are wild animals and they don't need a rowdy kid ruffling their feathers." He pointed a finger at her. "And be nice to the volunteers. You tend to roll your eyes when anyone tries to be nice to you. Don't think I haven't noticed."

"I promise!" Destiny said. Overcome with relief, she stood up from the table and gave Jake an awkward hug.

The following Monday, Destiny joined the staff for their morning meeting. They sat in the warehouse on folding chairs. Jake and Chrissy outlined the tasks that needed to be done and gave report on the status of each of the birds in their care.

Destiny was assigned the task of cleaning out two empty enclosures. Ruth, one of the older volunteers, came with her to show her how. She gave Destiny a pair of old leather gloves and a bucket. Ruth carried a rake and a shovel. "We keep it pretty natural out here," she said. "But we do need to get rid of what waste material we can." Destiny caught on quickly and soon Ruth left her to finish while she started on the next enclosure.

When Chrissy came out to check on her, Destiny didn't hear her coming. Destiny was talking and Chrissy looked around to see who she was talking to. No one was there.

"I don't know what you are complaining about," Destiny was saying. "You have everything you need here. There's plenty of food and water, and you are safe."

Chrissy looked closer. Destiny was standing next to one of their large flight enclosures. She was leaning her head against the wooden wall. A rather finicky golden eagle was inside the cage making a huge ruckus. Chrissy smiled. She made some noise as she walked closer. Destiny jumped and started raking the ground.

"How's it going out here?" Chrissy asked. "Are you bored yet?"

"Everything's fine," Destiny said, not looking up. "I'm almost done. What do I do next?"

Chrissy smiled. "I think that it's just about lunchtime. Shall we take a break?" Destiny nodded and picked up her bucket. They walked back inside together and went into the office. Jake was on the phone, so they sat down to wait for him. Without thinking, Destiny pulled her notebook out and opened it. She started drawing the eagle she had been talking to.

"What's this?" Chrissy asked, pointing to the notebook.

Destiny shrugged her shoulders. "Nothing."

Chrissy leaned over and looked closer. "You really have an eye for detail. I didn't know you could draw."

"It's no big deal," Destiny said. She put her hand over the page.

"I wish I could draw like that," Chrissy continued. "You make it look easy."

Destiny started to put the notebook in her pocket. Then she paused, pulled it out again, and offered it to Chrissy. "You can look at it if you want."

Chrissy took the notebook and slowly started turning pages. She recognized the significance of the offering. She didn't talk but examined the pages carefully. Jake finished his call and said, "What's this?" He scooted his chair closer to them.

"Our Destiny is an artist, Jake," Chrissy said. She turned the notebook so he could see it better.

Jake whistled. "Dang. This is really good! Hey, I recognize that old bird." The book was open to a drawing of the big barn owl. "That looks just like him!"

Destiny ducked her head to her chest and dug her toe into the carpet. She reached out and took the notebook back. She closed it and put it in her big pocket.

Chrissy and Jake exchanged a look. "Let's go get some lunch, shall we?" Jake said to break the awkward silence. The three of them stood up and filed out of the office.

That afternoon, Destiny helped Chrissy in the gift shop. They dusted the shelves and organized the books. Destiny spent a good deal of time organizing the bin of stuffed animals. She arranged them by family groups, putting the small ones in the front and the large ones in the back.

The next day, Chrissy watched Destiny as she worked with Randy, their resident handyman. She handed him nails as he repaired loose boards on one of the flight enclosures. Randy, a contractor by trade, switched spots with Destiny and had her climb up the ladder and hammer some of the nails. Chrissy smiled and went back to her desk. Destiny was slowly coming out of her shell.

Destiny's notebook became filled with detailed drawings of feathers and beaks and talons. She felt a connection with these animals that went beyond what other people experienced. She knew what it was like to be abandoned by her mother, starving and cold. She sympathized on a deep level with the ones that came in battered and bruised. She understood how they felt when they hid at the back of their enclosures or hissed when anyone came near them.

Jake spent a lot of time with Destiny, teaching her how to read the birds' body language. When the big barn owl opened his beak and started to breathe fast, she knew to back away and leave his area. The owl was trying to say, "Give me some space! I'm feeling stressed!"

Destiny, herself, was needing less space. She was opening up more to Chrissy and Jake. They were great at reading her body language as well. They knew when to leave her alone and give her space, but were always nearby to let her know that she wasn't alone. They also started to encourage her to talk, to start to heal. That hug she had given Jake was a big deal. It was the first time that Destiny had wanted physical contact of any kind.

Chapter 25

There was one room at the Rehab Center that was off-limits to Destiny, the Critical Care Room. This was where the birds were brought when they first arrived at the center. They were assessed and treated and kept in smaller enclosures to help them acclimate. It also gave them a quiet place to begin to heal.

The first twenty-four hours after a bird arrives at the center are critical to the bird's care. Very few people were allowed in the area. The fewer people who handled or were around the birds at this stage, the calmer the birds were. Jake and Chrissy were also afraid of scaring Destiny by seeing the condition some of the birds were in when they arrived. Some of them were hit by cars, some were poisoned or shot. They knew that Destiny had a traumatic past and didn't want her to go through any more.

"What's in there?" Destiny would ask. "Why won't you let me see?" Almost daily she begged to be allowed in. The answer was always no. They wouldn't even allow her to go in when the room was empty.

Destiny wasn't one to give up easily. She didn't throw a fit. Instead, she set her jaw and determined to prove to Jake and Chrissy that she was mature enough to handle whatever was inside. She started looking for ways to take on more responsibility and learn everything she could about caring for injured birds.

One day, Jake found Destiny standing in front of the Bird Status Board in the workroom. This large whiteboard contained all the notes on the birds that were at the center permanently as ambassadors that were ready to be taken out in public to an education function. Destiny was studying the board and writing things down in her journal.

"Whatcha doing?" Jake asked, setting down his leather gloves.

"Nothing," Destiny said, squinting up at the top of the board.

"You sure are writing a lot for doing nothing," he said. "Can I help you with something? Is there something new you want to learn?" He had come to appreciate how quickly Destiny picked up on things and was absorbing as much information about healing birds as she could.

Destiny tapped her pencil against her lips. "Um, maybe," she said. She pointed to an entry on the board next to one of the birds' identifiers. "Why is that bird listed as 'off handling'?"

Jake looked at where she was pointing. "That's our male American Kestrel. He injured his foot and so 'off handling' means that he won't do any training or any events until he heals. Sometimes they go 'off handling' when we work the birds a lot and they get stressed out from being around people too much. Kind of like giving them a vacation. These birds view people as predators, and when we put them in a noisy environment, like a school, it causes their heart rate to go up, and they try to run away."

Destiny nodded slowly. "Kind of like I do when people get too close to me," she said. "I know how they feel. Trapped. That's why I like to sit in the closet sometimes. It helps me calm down."

Jake patted her on the back. "Just like you."

"I have another question," Destiny said. "Why does that other one say 'now a Special Handling Bird'?"

Jake said, "That Red-Tailed Hawk does best with just one or two specially trained and skilled handlers. He doesn't trust people. He can go to events; he just has to be with the right person who is highly skilled at working with him."

Destiny wrote in her journal. Then she looked at Jake and said, "I guess that's kind of like me, too." She ducked her head. "Remember the time I hissed at you in the closet? I must be a Special Handling kid."

Jake smiled and hugged her. His mind replayed their first few days with Destiny. She had indeed acted like some of the birds did when they were brought to the Center. She was small and frightened and didn't want anyone to get close to her. He vividly remembered opening the closet door and getting hissed at. "You are very special, Destiny, but not that way. You've had some hard times and people have hurt you. You need some time to heal, just like these birds."

Destiny took a deep breath. "Can I help you with the Critical Care area, please? I know what these birds are going through and how they feel. I want to be there for them when they first get here. I can handle it, I promise." She looked up at him with big pleading eyes.

Jake shook his head. "Maybe someday, Destiny, but not now. You have to have a lot of special training, and besides, you aren't old enough."

Destiny's face fell and she started to leave.

Jake went on, "I have an idea. How about tomorrow you go with me to the flight enclosures and help me assess that other male kestrel that we've been treating. He's been getting very strong and I think we might be able to release him soon."

Destiny turned back around with a smile. "I'd rather do both. But, if I can't help in the Critical Care Room, I'd like to help the kestrel," she said. "I love that little guy. I call him Bob since he's always bobbing his head up and down. I love that he talks to me when I am by his enclosure. It makes me happy." She walked out with a bounce in her step.

Jake shook his head and smiled to himself. Looking at her now, he couldn't believe this was the same kid. This conversation would never have happened a few weeks ago. It was clear that she cared for these animals. She still had plenty of hard moments, to be sure, but they were slowly fading. This 'Special Handling Kid' was beginning to respond to them.

Chapter 26

Bright and early the next day, Destiny went out back with Jake. "Ok, Destiny, remember, don't lift that board until I say so," Jake said. She nodded quickly. They were standing outside one of the large flight enclosures behind the Center. The walls were twenty-foot-tall wooden fence panels. The roof was made of wood, as well. Inside the enclosure, sticking out of the walls were perches set at different heights. There were also some perches on the ground that looked a little like benches. A small reddish-brown bird with black lines on its wings was flitting from perch to perch. It had perfect form and it was impossible to tell that it had recently been hit by a car. Jake and Destiny watched it proudly through the cracks in the walls.

Destiny was crouched next to a small box set into the wall against the ground. The front of the box had a sliding panel. She had her hand on a loop in the sliding panel, waiting for Jake's signal. Jake waited until the kestrel had settled onto one of the perches and was facing towards them.

"Now!" he said softly, so as not to startle the kestrel.

Destiny lifted the panel and shook the box. A small mouse scurried into the enclosure. It stopped for a moment and looked around. Then it took off running towards a pile of corn that Jake had left for it. The kestrel spotted the mouse immediately. Both Jake and Destiny held their breath. Would the kestrel recognize the mouse as food? If it did, would it be able to catch it? The bird had suffered a head injury. Everyone was afraid that it would be too severely injured to hunt for itself in the wild. Its recovery had been quick, though, due to the expert care it had received, so Jake and Chrissy were hopeful that he would be able to be released.

The kestrel watched the mouse carefully. It shifted its weight on the perch. It bobbed its head to zone in on the mouse. Suddenly it took off across the enclosure. Talons outstretched; the mouse never had a chance. Destiny wanted to cheer but held it in by covering her mouth with her hands. She knew better than to startle the bird.

Walking back to the main building, Destiny couldn't contain her excitement any more. "Did you see how quickly Bob saw that mouse? Did you see how he focused on it by bobbing his head? Did you see how straight he flew? That was amazing!" She was hanging on Jake's arm and jumping up and down. "Did he pass his test? Do we get to release him, then?"

"You bet. That was his last test. We have been doing this exercise with him for a week now, and he has never once missed a meal. I say he is ready to go back to the wild. Do you want to help?" Jake asked, like he didn't already know the answer. He had never seen Destiny act this animated before.

"Can I? Yes, please, I want to, very much!"

Jake grinned and said, "Let's go tell Chrissy and the rest of the staff the good news." Before he had finished speaking, Destiny had let go of his arm and rushed to the door of the building.

The next morning, Destiny woke up early. She couldn't wait to get back to the Rehab Center and help Bob get back into the wild. She went to her closet and pulled on her favorite jeans, a tee-shirt, and then grabbed her green sweatshirt. She held it in her hands for a minute, then put it gently back on the shelf. Instead, she put on the new purple down vest that Chrissy had given her for Christmas. This was a special occasion.

She skipped down the stairs and into the kitchen. Chrissy and Jake weren't up yet, so she poured herself a glass of orange juice and made some toast. Her stomach was full of butterflies. Her notebook was sitting on the table, where she'd left it the night before. Flipping to the page she'd been working on, she picked up her pencil. The drawing showed Bob, the kestrel, with wings outstretched and talons spread, getting ready to grab the mouse. Destiny bent her head over the picture and started shading the tail feathers.

She was so absorbed in her work that she didn't hear the couple come into the kitchen. The clink of a cup startled her and she looked up. Chrissy was leaning on the door jamb with her arms crossed. She had a smile on her face as she watched Destiny. Jake was pouring a cup of coffee.

"Good morning, Sunshine," Chrissy said, crossing the floor. She pulled out a chair and sat next to Destiny. "Excited about this morning?"

Destiny nodded her head vigorously. "I can't wait to see Bob fly into the blue sky!"

Chrissy nodded toward the drawing. "Can I take a look?"

Destiny pushed the notebook towards Chrissy. "Wow, Destiny, this is amazing. You have captured the kestrel perfectly. If you would let me, I'd like to frame this picture and put it in the office at the Rehab Center."

Destiny's eyes went big. She had never thought of her drawings as being for others to see. She did them for her own enjoyment. Shaking her head, she said, "It's not finished yet. Besides, this is just notebook paper."

"Would you make one for me to frame if I got you some art paper?" Chrissy asked.

Destiny ducked her head. "Maybe," she said, softly.

When they arrived at the Rehab Center, the rest of the staff was standing out front, waiting for them, even the ones who had the day off. No one wanted to miss this special occasion. It felt like a party.

Jake found a large crate and put an old soft towel in the bottom. Then, he and Chrissy put on long leather gloves and took the crate to the enclosure. It took them a long time to corner and capture the kestrel. Once he was in the crate, he made his displeasure known, loudly. They put the crate in the back of the Suburban and placed a blanket over the top to keep the kestrel calm.

Jake, Chrissy, Destiny and two of the volunteers climbed into the Suburban. Destiny climbed into the back seat so that she could reach over and keep a hand on Bob's crate. Somehow, she thought that it might help keep him calm. The rest of the staff and volunteers filled two more vehicles and the caravan left the parking lot.

They drove north out of town and kept going for what seemed like forever to Destiny. She watched out the window and hummed along with the radio. Finally, Jake slowed and turned onto a dirt road. The landscape was full of rolling hills covered in brown grass. Cottonwood trees with bare winter branches stood over a small stream not far away. There were fence posts lining one side of the road. Pulling off the road onto the grass, the vehicles stopped.

Everyone got out and readied their cameras. Jake went around to the back of the Suburban and pulled the crate out. He set it on the ground. He put on his thick leather gloves. Chrissy took the blanket off of the crate. Opening the metal door, Jake reached inside. The tiny predator started making high-pitched sounds to make his displeasure known. He flapped his wings and pecked at Jake's gloves.

When Jake finally stood up and turned around, all you could see of the kestrel was his slate blue and rust-colored head. He continued to voice his displeasure at this rude treatment. Jake cradled the bird close to his body and held it still. The staff started discussing which direction to release the bird and their predictions of where it would go.

Destiny stood next to Chrissy and tucked her hand into the crook of Chrissy's arm. She had a lump in her throat. This was an exciting moment, but she also felt a little like she was losing a friend.

Jake cleared his throat. "I always get choked up at times like this. Thank you to everyone for your hard work. You made this moment possible. Are we ready?"

The moment had come. Everyone counted down, "Three...two...one!"

Jake released the bird into the air. It spread its wings and flew away. It turned and came back, flying in a circle above their heads as if to say, "Thanks for everything!" And then it was gone. They watched until Bob was a tiny speck on the horizon, and then disappeared.

"Be free," Destiny whispered.

The crowd cheered and clapped their hands. Destiny noticed that she wasn't the only one wiping tears from her cheeks. She put her head on Chrissy's arm and held on. Chrissy wrapped her other arm around Destiny. They stayed that way for a long minute before Destiny found her composure.

Chapter 27

Life settled into a comfortable routine for Destiny. When school started up again, she made more of an effort to get along with her classmates and her teachers. She took a lesson from her friend Bob, the kestrel, and looked at school as her flight enclosure. She just had to show these people that she could do the things they were asking, and then they would let her go. She still watched the clock and bolted for the door when the final bell rang.

Every day there were new challenges at the Rehab Center. Destiny loved every minute of it. She couldn't wait to see what new birds had been brought in, and pitch in wherever Jake and Chrissy would allow.

One Sunday morning, when the Prestons and Destiny were relaxing at home, Jake's phone rang. It was their turn to be on call for the Rehab Center. After listening for several minutes, he said, "Thanks for the call. We'll be there in about 30 minutes."

He signed off and turned to Chrissy. "That was a rancher who lives up north of here.

He was pulling hay bales from a stack and a bunch of baby owls fell out. Sounds like barn owls to me."

"Road trip!" Chrissy said. She, Jake and Destiny piled into the Suburban and headed to the Center. They went into the warehouse and began gathering equipment. Chrissy told Destiny to find a large crate and a towel while she thawed out some frozen mice.

They headed back out to the Suburban with their supplies. They drove out of town and across the plains. The cottonwoods they passed by the river had small, bright green leaves.

They turned onto a bumpy dirt road and followed it for several miles. "Are you sure you know where this place is?" Chrissy asked. "I think we're lost."

Jake said, "I'm following this guy's directions. I think we're almost there. Yep, there's the red barn he told me about." They had just come over the crest of a hill. Nestled at the bottom were a white house and a big old-fashioned barn.

There were tractors and farm equipment lined up beside it.

Several dogs came out of the yard and started barking at them. They stayed in the Suburban until a man came out of the house and shooed the dogs away. He was tall and skinny and wore a weathered blue button-down shirt and jeans with a soiled John Deere ball cap.

He walked over to the driver's door. Jake let the window down. "They won't hurt you none. They're just the welcoming committee." He stuck out his large, work-worn hand. "I'm Pete Johannsen. You Jake?"

Jake shook his hand. "Yep. This is Chrissy and Destiny. Want to show me those owlets?" He opened the door and stepped out. Chrissy and Destiny went to the back of the Suburban and grabbed the crate and some gloves.

Pete led them to the back of the barn where hay had been stacked higher than their heads. They walked around to the back side of the stack and saw some wooden pallets propped up like a fence.

"Didn't want the dogs to get to them," Pete explained. He moved one of the pallets and Destiny could see several little balls of white fluff in some loose hay.

Jake grinned. "I like the way you think, Pete. Thanks for looking out for the little guys."

"Well, the way I figure it, owls do us a favor by eating mice and snakes and such. This is the least I could do for them. Circle of life kinda thing, you know." Pete took off his cap and scratched his head. "You gonna want to put them back in the haystack?"

Jake looked around. "Looks like the nest was destroyed when you pulled the bales out. Most likely the parents won't come back and feed them. We'll take them back to the Center and hand-raise them. When they are old enough, we'll bring them back out here and set them loose."

Pete nodded. "Sounds like a plan. Give me a call when you're ready to come back. I'll make sure the dogs are locked up."

Jake put on the leather gloves and picked up the owlets one by one and placed them into the crate. Destiny crouched by his side. "They look like baby pterodactyls," she said, giggling. The owlets peered out at her with dark eyes.

"We are going to have to raise them, now," Chrissy said. "It's going to be a lot of work. The first few days are going to be hard. We have to feed them without them imprinting."

"What's that?" Destiny asked.

"Imprinting where a young animal thinks the thing with eyes that brings it food is its parent. If it imprints on a human, it won't be able to survive in the wild. We want as many of our birds to return to the wild as possible, so we have to take steps to make sure they don't think we are their mommies."

"How do you do that? Dress up like a giant owl?" Destiny smiled at the thought of Jake with a beak and feathers.

Chrissy laughed. "Close. No owl costume. We wear camouflage and try to look like a bush or a tree. We put a stuffed adult owl that is the same species in the enclosure with the owlets. Like this one." Chrissy showed her the stuffed owl that she had brought with them. "When we get back to the Center, we'll use a hand puppet and tweezers to feed the owlets. That way the owlets think that the adult owl brought them the food. They'll spend the first few days in the Critical Care Room until they get stronger, and then we put them into our foster care program."

They walked back to the house with Pete and said good-bye.

"I didn't know owls had foster care, just like people do," Destiny said. She looked thoughtful.

Chrissy said, "We have the perfect foster parent for them back at the Center."

As soon as the babies were able to hold themselves upright again, Jake moved them in with the old barn owl that Destiny called Grandpa. Whenever someone found a barn owl chick that had been blown out of its nest, they brought it to Grandpa to raise. He had a way with them. He taught them how to hunt, how to protect themselves from predators, and he even had a signature hoot for them. These chicks were no different. The old owl immediately started making noises deep in his throat, sort of like the owl version of purring. He used his beak to gather them under his wings. Destiny, Jake, and Chrissy stood at a distance and watched as the old owl took a dead mouse that Jake had placed in the enclosure, ripped it into small pieces and fed it to the eager owlets.

"They are going to be OK, now that the barn owl is on the case," Chrissy whispered to Destiny. "He has raised more owlets than I can remember. Every one of them has been released back into the wild and has done fine. He seems to understand that these little ones need extra special care and he is so patient with them."

Destiny whispered back, "Kind of like how you are with me." She smiled up at Chrissy and hugged her.

Jake and Chrissy locked eyes over Destiny's head. They both had tears in their eyes.

Chapter 28

As the semester progressed, Destiny found it a little easier to pay attention to her teachers every day. She stopped ignoring them and tried to listen. She realized that they weren't trying to pick on her. One day, she actually raised her hand to answer a math problem.

"Well, well, well," Mr. Petra said. "Look who showed up to work today. Class, can we show Destiny some love?" The whole class clapped for Destiny. She ducked her head and her cheeks went pink.

During independent work time, one of her classmates came and sat next to her. "I like your shirt," the girl said. "I'm Amy."

"Thanks," Destiny mumbled. She looked down to see what Amy was talking about. She hadn't worn her oversized sweatshirt in weeks. Today she was wearing a shirt that showed a falcon in flight.

At lunch, Destiny was walking to her usual table by the wall when she heard someone call her name. Turning, she saw Amy and another girl waving her over. Destiny nearly tripped over her own two feet. She caught herself and walked slowly to their table.

"Come sit with us," Amy said. "Britany, scoot over." Britany scooted and Destiny sat down. She felt awkward and didn't know what to say. As it turned out, she didn't have to worry about it because Britany liked to talk, and Destiny never got a word in edgewise.

That afternoon, her class went to the library. Destiny wasn't in the mood to pick a book, so she wandered around, pretending to look. She found herself in a section she had never been in before. There were large, hardbacked books about all kinds of animals on the shelves. The librarian had chosen a few to display on the top of the bookcase. One was called, "Birds of Prey: North America". She pulled it down and opened it. There were full-color photographs of many of the birds that were at the Rehab Center, plus many that Destiny had never seen or heard of. Quickly, she walked to the circulation desk and checked it out. She sat at a table and began to read. It was slow going, Destiny struggled with most of the words, but she was determined to read it. This book promised so much in the way of information that she wanted to know.

That night, she took the book home. After dinner, she sat on the couch and put her feet up. Chrissy wandered in and sat next to her. "What's this?" Chrissy asked.

"I found this book about raptors in the school library today. I'm trying to read it, but it's hard," Destiny said. She showed Chrissy some of the pictures.

Chrissy said, "Then let's read it together." They read the book page by page and studied the pictures. Destiny stopped after each page and asked Chrissy question after question. Jake heard them and came into the living room. He plopped himself down on the other side of Destiny.

"I want to read, too," he said. "No one invited me to this party."

Just then, Jake's phone rang. He had left it on the counter in the kitchen. Groaning, he hauled himself off the couch and went to get it. Destiny and Chrissy kept reading. Jake's phone went off constantly, sometimes the volunteers at the Rehab Center had questions, sometimes it was the emergency helpline. Jake was on call more often than not.

Something in Jake's tone caught Destiny and Chrissy's attention. They looked up as he came into the room. "Thanks for calling," he said and hung up.

He sat back down on the couch and took Destiny's book from her. Gently laying it on the coffee table, he said, "That was Miss Laura. She has some news. They found your mother and she's been getting some help. She's been taking parenting classes. She wants to see you."

Destiny covered her face with her hands. She tried to take deep breaths, but it felt like a boa constrictor had wrapped itself around her chest. She pictured the great horned owl when it started to breathe through its mouth.

She wanted to see her mother, but images from her past flooded her mind. Sleeping on a filthy mattress, shivering with cold. Her stomach hurting from hunger. Sounds of angry men yelling from the other room. Wandering the streets, looking for food. Avoiding home because her mother was in a bad mood, or the people she brought home didn't like kids.

"What do you mean, she wants to see me? She abandoned me," Destiny asked in a very small voice. "Does she want to take me home with her?" She had pulled her knees up to her chest and was hugging them with her arms. She put her face down against them and squeezed her eyes shut.

Jake put an arm around her from one side, and Chrissy did the same from the other side. Destiny was as stiff as a board. Jake clenched his jaw to choke down the angry words he wanted to speak about anyone who could make her react this way. Taking a deep breath, he said, "No, sweetie, you are not going to go home with her. But you do have to go see her. Miss Laura is required by the court to let her see you."

"Is she coming here?" Destiny asked, her voice muffled by her knees.

"Absolutely not," Jake said. "We will take you to Miss Laura's office. They have a room there for parents to visit their kids. Miss Laura will stay in the room with you the whole time."

"When?" came the small voice.

"Tomorrow at 10 o'clock. You will visit her for an hour, and then we will bring you home again."

Destiny had retreated back into her shell. She ran upstairs and put on her sweatshirt. She wanted to run away. She hid in the closet, but Chrissy and Jake coaxed her back out. They let her keep her sweatshirt on to sleep in. Chrissy tucked her into the bed.

"Chrissy," Destiny said.

"Yes?"

Destiny paused and squirmed. "Do you think you could stay with me tonight? I don't want to be alone in the dark."

Chrissy climbed onto the fluffy purple comforter and lay down next to Destiny. Destiny rolled onto her side and buried her face against Chrissy's chest. Chrissy wrapped her arms around the little girl and held her tight. Chrissy started singing a lullaby that she remembered her mother singing to her when she felt afraid. Destiny closed her eyes and eventually dozed off. Chrissy didn't move. She lay there in the moonlight, staring at the wall covered with drawings of birds. Tears streamed across her cheeks and onto the pillow.

Chapter 29

The next day Chrissy and Jake came to the school and signed Destiny out to take her to Laura's office. They drove across town and parked in front of the big glass building where they had first met.

Inside, they sat in the lobby and waited. The elevator doors opened and Laura stepped out. She led them to a different part of the building that had a waiting room with several conference rooms opening from it. Jake and Chrissy sat on an orange couch in the waiting area while Laura led Destiny into one of the conference rooms. Destiny walked to the doorway and stopped.

Her mother was sitting at the small table, facing them. She was thinner than Destiny remembered her. Her clothes looked brand new. She had on a black v necked sweater and her dishwater blonde hair had been curled. She had black eyeliner around her eyes.

Laura stood behind Destiny and put her hands on Destiny's shoulders.

She whispered in Destiny's ear, "It's OK. I'll be here the whole time with you." She managed to get Destiny across the room and set her on a chair opposite her mother. Then Laura went back and closed the door and sat in a chair right next to it.

Destiny looked at her mother, then stuck her hands into her pocket and slumped in her chair.

"Hi, Destiny. How are you?" Paula said. Her hands were on the table and she twisted them together.

Destiny shrugged her shoulders and looked at the floor.

Her mother tried again. "You look good."

Destiny ignored her and turned sideways in her chair. She continued to study the floor. Paula got up and came around the table. She knelt in front of Destiny. Destiny swiveled and faced the other way. She felt her mother's hand on her back. She stood up quickly and went to the door. "Can I leave now?" she said to Laura.

"No, Destiny. We need to stay. Your mother is trying to be nice. At least talk to her." Laura gestured to the table. "Tell your mom what you've been doing lately."

"Why," Destiny demanded. "She's only being nice to me because you are here. She doesn't care about me."

"That's not true," Paula said in a sugary sweet voice. "I do care about you. I love you." She approached Destiny with her arms out, ready to hug her. She came close enough for Destiny to smell cigarette smoke, then Destiny bolted to the other side of the table.

"STAY AWAY FROM ME!" Her face flushed and she started breathing hard. Angry tears ran down her face as she shouted. She turned around and stood in the corner of the room, her hot forehead touching the cool wall.

Paula, in a not-so-sweet voice, said, "Look, D., I'm trying to change. I made some mistakes and I'm trying to fix them. Would you listen?"

Destiny spoke to the wall. "Go away. I hate you. You don't love me."

"Hey, knock it off, Destiny," her mother's tone became ice cold. "You listen to me. I landed in this trouble because of you." Paula's face had gone dark.

Laura stood up and said, "That's enough, Paula. You need to leave right now."

Paula grabbed her purse off the back of the chair and said, "Ungrateful little bitch!" She stormed out of the room and slammed the door.

Destiny turned around, went over to the table and pulled out one of the chairs. She crawled under the table and huddled there, hugging her knees. She closed her eyes and started rocking.

When Jake and Chrissy saw Paula come raging out of the room, they stood up. They ran to the conference room and looked at Laura. She pointed under the table. Jake pulled another chair away and crawled under the table with Destiny. Chrissy followed him and they put their arms around her.

"Can we go see the birds?" came Destiny's muffled voice.

"Of course," Chrissy said gently, and they all crawled out from under the table.

They drove straight to the Rehab Center and Destiny walked through the building and out the back door. She reached Grandpa's enclosure and leaned her head against the rough cold wood. She stood there, watching the owlets waddle around, Grandpa preening himself, and waited for the fire inside herself to cool. Grandpa glanced at her, tilted his head from side to side, and started making a purring noise deep in his throat. All the owlets came wandering over and he tucked them under his wings.

Jake and Chrissy stood next to the building, watching her. Chrissy reached for Jake's hand. They didn't know how to comfort Destiny, but it seemed that the owl did. Chrissy wondered if Destiny would ever recover from the wounds she carried.

The next week, it took some serious convincing to get Destiny back to Laura for another visit.

At breakfast, Chrissy said, "We'll be at school at 9:30 to pick you up. We have to be at Miss Laura's office at 10:00."

"I'm not going," Destiny said, staring into her cereal bowl.

"I'm afraid it's not a choice," Jake said. "These visits are court-ordered for your mother. You have to go. Maybe this time it will be better."

Destiny stood up. "It won't be better. She is a two-faced liar and I hate her!" Her hands were clenched and her face was red. "I'm not going and you can't make me."

Chrissy said, "Destiny, we have to take you. If we don't, we could get in trouble with the courts and they could take you away from us. Please go. We don't want to lose you."

Destiny looked from Chrissy to Jake. They had the same look on their faces that they had last week when they thought they were going to lose the hawk who had lead poisoning.

"Fine," she said, sitting back down. "But I'm not going to talk to her."

Chrissy let her breath out. "That's up to you, Destiny. You just need to go and make an effort."

Destiny left the table and went to get her backpack. When she came back downstairs, she was wearing her green sweatshirt. Chrissy raised her eyebrows but didn't say anything.

When they arrived at Laura's office, they checked in and sat on the black chairs in the lobby. Laura came out of the elevator and led them to the now-familiar waiting area. "Your mother isn't here yet, Destiny," she said. "But I'm sure she's on her way."

They sat together and made small talk. Laura kept checking her watch. Finally, she excused herself and went back to the lobby. Destiny had her hands in her pocket, rubbing her pencil. Chrissy picked up an old magazine and flipped pages without reading them. Jake stood up and paced to the window on the far wall. His hands were balled up in his pockets.

They heard footsteps and looked up. Laura came back with a grim look on her face. "No sign of her yet." She sat between Chrissy and Destiny. They waited the full hour, but Paula never showed up.

Laura looked worried and angry at the same time. "I'll be in touch when I figure out what happened," she said.

As they walked to the Suburban, Destiny said, "I told you she didn't care." She climbed in, pulled her hood up, and slammed the door. Crossing her arms, she stared out the window.

Jake climbed in and started the car. "You doing OK, Destiny?"

"I'm fine. Just leave me alone." Destiny pulled the hood up and leaned her forehead against the window.

Jake backed out and headed for the Rehab Center.

"School's the other way, Jake," Chrissy said, pointing.

"I think someone needs some owl therapy," Jake said.

Chrissy nodded.

Destiny didn't say a word the whole trip. When they crunched into the parking lot, Destiny practically threw herself out of the car and ran to the door. By the time Jake and Chrissy got inside, she was nowhere to be seen. They followed their instinct and stepped out the back door in time to hear Destiny talking to the old barn owl.

"...feel like a piece of trash. She only wanted to see me to get people off her back. When everyone's watching she can be nice, but I know how she is when she is alone. Once she gets what she wants, she'll throw me away again."

Jake and Chrissy could hear soft sobs. Jake stayed outside while Chrissy quietly went back inside and shut the door. She pulled out her phone and called Miss Laura. "Hey, Laura. Any news on the Paula front? We decided not to take Destiny to school after what happened. She's pretty shaken up. She is experiencing her mother's abandonment all over again."

"No news to report. It's like she vanished into thin air again. I've tried all the places I can think of. I'll keep trying. I think that it is imperative that we get Destiny into some counseling immediately. I know a woman who specializes in helping foster children and has experience with abandonment issues. I'll text you her information," Laura said. She sounded tired.

Chrissy said, "Thanks, Laura. I know you are doing all you can. It breaks my heart to see this little girl trying to shoulder heavy issues. No child should have to go through things like this. Her mom has so much baggage to deal with that has nothing to do with her daughter. But Destiny doesn't see it that way. She thinks this is her fault and that she caused all this."

Ms. Sanders said, "I'm right there with you. That's why I do this job. Someone has to be their voice. Hey, I have an idea. I spoke with Susan Moore on the phone yesterday. She's the foster mom that had Destiny before you. She asked how Destiny was doing. She sounded upbeat and said that her cancer treatments are going well. Maybe she would be up for a little visit from Destiny. I know it would do Destiny good."

"That's a great idea!" Chrissy said. "Let's set it up for Saturday."

When Saturday morning came, Chrissy knocked on Destiny's door and said, "We need to run some errands today. Get your clothes on and meet me in the kitchen."

Destiny came downstairs and sat at the table. She put her head down on her arms. "Do I have to go? Why do I have to go? Can't I just stay home and veg out?"

Jake put his coffee cup in the dishwasher. "Sorry, Champ. Chrissy says we all have to go. I don't want to go either, but if we get it over quickly, we can come home and veg the rest of the day."

They fed her, got her into the Suburban and started down the highway. "Where are we going?" Destiny asked. "Is it an injured bird?" She looked behind her in the cargo area. "It can't be. We didn't bring a crate." She drummed her fingers on the door. "Is it another rehab center? An animal hospital? What?"

When Chrissy and Jake wouldn't say, she slumped in her seat and said, "They found my mother again, didn't they? You're taking me to see her, aren't you?"

"Nope," Chrissy said, "I would never keep something like that a secret from you. But we do have a surprise for you!" A short time later, Jake pulled the car to the curb in front of a small white house that had big pine trees in front. Destiny sat up and looked around. Nothing looked familiar.

"Wait for it," Jake said. He drummed his hands on the steering wheel.

Suddenly the front door flew open and a little girl in a pink dress came running out, followed by a giant shaggy white dog. They came barreling toward the car. The girl was laughing and the dog was barking furiously.

Destiny stared for a split second, then frantically tried to unbuckle her seat belt. The harder she tried, the more she fumbled. Finally, she managed to unclip herself and opened the door. Jumping out, she yelled, "Julie!" and hugged her foster sister. They jumped around on the sidewalk together until Jackson knocked them onto the grass while trying to lick both girls at the same time. They lay there giggling and fending off the fluffy white dog.

Hearing car doors slam, Jackson stopped his slobbery assault and turned his attention back to the Suburban. He ran over and placed his front paws on Jake's shoulders and licked his face. Jake pushed him down, laughing.

"Jackson, come here!" yelled Derrick, coming out of the house with his grandparents. The big dog loped to his side, wagging his tail. Introductions were made, Jackson was banished to the backyard, and everyone made their way into the house.

Grandpa Ben led the way to the back of the house and into a sunroom that was filled with white wicker furniture, covered in cheerful yellow cushions. Sitting on a couch by the window, they found Susan. She was pale and thin. A blanket covered her lap and wrapped around her legs. Her head was covered with a red and white striped bandanna. Her skin was paper-thin and had a yellowish tinge to it.

"Oh, Destiny! I'm so glad you are here! Come give me a hug!" Susan opened her arms and Destiny ran to her. Susan started crying. Destiny tried not to, but ended up with tears on her cheeks, too. "I have missed you so much," Susan said. She held Destiny for a long time. "I am so sorry that you had to leave us." She lifted the blanket and pulled Destiny to her side, wrapping them both in its warmth. She pressed her lips to Destiny's forehead. Looking up, she saw Jake and Chrissy standing in the doorway with Grandpa Ben.

Without letting go of Destiny, Susan extended her thin hand to Jake and Chrissy. "It's so nice to meet you. Please sit down. I want to hear all about you." Turning to Destiny, she said, "You have grown so much! What have you been up to? I want to hear everything."

"Jake and Chrissy work at this cool place where they help birds and send them back into the wild," Destiny said. "I get to help, too. Well, not with the cool stuff, I'm not old enough yet. I sweep and clean cages and cut up their food and stuff. We have an old owl that helps raise babies and everything."

Jake said, "We are at the Raptor Rehabilitation Center. Destiny is a big help. She is a fast learner and works hard. I think we have a junior rehabber on our hands."

Julie was dancing around her mother and Destiny. "Mama, can I show Destiny the backyard?"

"Of course, you can," Susan said, "if Destiny wants to."

Part of Destiny never wanted to leave the warm embrace of Susan's arms, but the other part of her wanted to run around the yard with Julie and Jackson, just like they used to do. Julie took Destiny's hand and tugged. "Please? Pretty please?" she begged.

"Ok, ok, I'm coming," Destiny said. She followed Julie out the side door.

The adults sat and watched the kids play for a few minutes. Then Susan turned to Chrissy and Jake and asked, "How is she doing, really? I've been worried about her. I felt terrible having to send her away. She is so very fragile on the inside, but tough on the outside."

Chrissy nodded. "I totally agree with you. She puts up such high walls to protect herself. We are seeing some cracks in the wall, though." She went on to tell Susan about the visit with Destiny's mother and the abandonment issues that came up. "Laura has suggested that we find a therapist for Destiny who deals specifically with foster children."

Nodding her head, Susan said, "I agree. That would be good for her. Now, tell me more about this bird hospital you run. That sounds interesting."

Jake shared stories about how Destiny was bonding with the birds in their care and how impressed they were with her drawing abilities.

An hour flew by. Chrissy noticed that Susan was beginning to close her eyes more and that her smile seemed strained. She bumped Jake with her elbow and said, "We'd better get going. We have a long drive to get back home. Thank you so much for letting us come over. This visit has been so good for Destiny. I know that she misses your family so much. Maybe we can come again another time." They stood up and shook hands with Grandpa Ben and Grandma Lucy. They called the girls in from the backyard and had Destiny say her good-byes.

"Do we have to go so soon?" Destiny asked, disappointed.

"We'll come to visit another time, OK?" Chrissy said gently. "Maybe we could have them come over to see the Rehab Center sometime. You could be the tour guide. Would you like that?"

"That would be awesome," Destiny said. She hugged Julie and Jackson. She even gave Derrick an awkward side hug and he patted her on the back. She ran over to Susan and hugged her, too. "Would you come and visit us?"

"Of course, we will," Susan said, hugging her back. "I'm so glad you came today. Now that I know where you are and that you are safe, I feel much better. I'll call you, too." The circles under her eyes belied the bright smile she gave Destiny.

Chapter 30

Early the next day, an urgent call came into the Rehab Center. A truck driver from a local gravel pit had found an osprey just inside their gates that morning when they came to work. He told them that the bird was alive, but wouldn't move.

Jake and Chrissy looked at each other in alarm.

"What's wrong?" Destiny asked, coming into the office. She had just finished checking on the owlets and was looking for a snack.

"We have an injured osprey to go get," Jake started. "They are the hardest bird to take care of in captivity. They almost never survive. I've never had a successful case in my life." While he talked, he moved quickly around the office, gathering equipment. Chrissy joined him and Destiny did, too.

"What can I do to help?" Destiny asked.

"Go grab one of those old blankets and a large carrier, please," Jake said as he grabbed his car keys and headed out the door.

When they arrived at the gates to the quarry, a large man wearing a white hardhat and a dark blue shirt was waiting for them.

Jake rolled down the window. "Are you Mike?" he asked.

"I am. The birds just over there," the man said, pointing to a clump of wild grass just off the road.

Jake and Chrissy jumped out of the Suburban and followed him. Standing among the grass was a large white and gray bird. Its feathers were rumpled looking and it was leaning to one side.

"I just found out that he's been here since last night," Mike said, shaking his head. "One of the other drivers told me he saw the bird when he left around 6. I don't know why he didn't call it in. I guess he didn't know what kind of bird it was."

Jake's heart skipped a beat. "He's been here for over twelve hours now. That lessens his odds for survival even more. We'd better hurry if we want to save this poor guy." He rushed back to the Suburban and pulled out the old blanket. He came back over and walked a wide circle around the bird to get behind it. Moving slowly, he walked up to the bird with the blanket open wide. He gently placed it over the bird and folded the edges up around it.

Destiny held her breath. She backed up against Chrissy, who put her arms around her. This bird was obviously in a lot of pain. She knew that Jake was being careful, but she could hardly stand still. Once she knew the bird was safely captured, she ran and brought the carrier to Jake. He put the bird inside, blanket and all. The bird was so weak, it didn't put up any fight. He put it in the back seat and climbed in beside it. Destiny hopped in on the other side and Chrissy drove them back to the Rehab Center.

"Why did you put a blanket over the bird?" Destiny asked. Her arm was draped over the carrier. "Why don't ospreys survive when they get caught?"

Jake said, "They get way more stressed out than other birds do. It causes their hearts to beat so fast and they breathe so fast that their bodies just can't take it. Putting the blanket over him keeps him calmer because he can't see, and also prevents him from flapping around and hurting himself worse. We're also dealing with a bird who is dehydrated and close to starving. There's a good chance he's been badly injured, judging from the way he was leaning and didn't fight me. This guy has a lot of strikes against him already. We're going to have to work very hard to help him.''

Destiny held the door open when they arrived at the center. Jake and Chrissy rushed the bird into the Critical Care room and carefully examined its leg and wing. The wing was badly broken. They gave the bird some pain medication and inserted an IV for fluids. Its leg was dislocated, but they were able to put it back in the socket. Then they bandaged the broken wing and secured it to the bird's side so that it couldn't move it at all.

To keep the osprey still and quiet, they put him in the smallest cage they had and covered it with a blanket. They checked the room temperature and adjusted it to make it a little warmer.

Coming out of the Critical Care Room, they saw Destiny pacing in the hallway. She rushed up to Jake and asked, ''How is he doing?'' Her face looked pained and concerned. Jake and Chrissy had never seen such emotion from her before.

''Honestly, Destiny, I don't know, but we've done everything we can do to help him. Only time will tell. He's bandaged up, he's quiet, and we've given him fluids and pain medication. That's about all we can do for him at the moment. It's up to him now.''

''No, it isn't,'' Destiny said, shaking her head and crossing her arms.

Chrissy asked, ''What do you mean? There isn't anything more we can do except give him time.''

Destiny shook her head again. ''I thought of something else we could try. I know how it feels to be stressed out like that. I've felt like my heart is going to beat out of my chest, too. Being in a dark, close space can help, but it doesn't change the fact that he is in here, not out there, where he comes from.''

Jake asked, ''What's your idea, Destiny?'' He stuck his hands in his pockets.

''What if we put speakers next to his carrier and played sounds from where he comes from. Then it wouldn't seem so stressful. Maybe he'd think he was in his own nest."

Jake thought for a minute, then nodded his head. "It couldn't hurt. I think we have a CD of nature sounds around here somewhere from when we did our Halloween Open House last year. Thanks for the suggestion, Destiny. I'll look for it after I call the fish hatchery." He headed toward the office.

"The fish hatchery?" Destiny said. She ran to catch up with him. "What do you need to call them for?"

"Osprey only eat fish, Destiny. If we want this guy to have the best chance to make it, we need to give him his exact diet." He sat down at his desk and picked up the phone.

After about two weeks in the Critical Care Room, Destiny watched as Jake and Chrissy moved the osprey to one of the large outdoor enclosures. She crossed her fingers and held her breath. She wanted to see him fly, now that his bandages had been removed. He was certainly making a lot more noise than he did when they first found him. When Jake opened the carrier, the osprey just hopped and fluttered his wings to move away from the humans, but after several attempts, he managed to make it to one of the lower perches.

Jake was pleased with the osprey's progress. The fact that he was still alive was a miracle in itself. Over the next couple of days, they watched the osprey carefully. His appetite remained good and he was adept at tearing apart the dead fish that they placed in his enclosure. He started stretching out his wings and making short flights from the lowest perches across the ground. On the third day, he took off and flew the entire length of the enclosure.

The osprey grew stronger. He swooped and dove. He banked his turns sharply as if his wing and leg had never been injured. "I think he's fine. We don't have any way to test his hunting capabilities, though. I think it's time to get him back to his home ground," Jake said. Jake knew that the sooner they could release it, the better. Catching the osprey was not an easy task. He wanted nothing to do with humans and tried very hard to let Jake know that he didn't like him. He bit and screeched and wriggled when Jake finally was able to wrap the blanket around the bird. He was very careful not to bend any of the feathers, as this could affect the osprey's ability to fly. Jake grinned the whole time. So did Chrissy and Destiny. The osprey had his fight back.

"Let's take him back to where we found him," Destiny said. She clasped her hands and hopped up and down.

Jake opted to hold the bird for the short drive. He didn't want the osprey to have another opportunity to injure itself on the trip. They stopped the Suburban at the edge of a lake that was near the gravel pit. Jake unwrapped the wriggling bird and released him. The osprey took off like a shot. He made a sharp turn and came back across the lake. Then they watched as he suddenly plunged down into the water with a big splash. Seconds later he came back up with a fish in his talons. Jake, Chrissy, and Destiny cheered.

"That was better than a Superbowl touchdown," Jake said, high-fiving Destiny and Chrissy.

Chapter 31

A week later, Laura called. She had found a therapist for Destiny. That night, after dinner, Jake and Chrissy sat down with Destiny and told her about it.

"Destiny," Chrissy started, "Miss Laura called today. She told us about a lady who helps kids. She wants you to visit with her. We want to go, too."

Destiny furrowed her brow. She picked up a colored pencil. "Helps kids with what? I don't need any help."

"We want you to get help dealing with all your feelings about your mom. She knows good ways to help kids who go through stressful times, like you have," Jake said. He picked up a pencil and played with it.

"I don't want to talk about those things," Destiny said. She continued shading with her pencil and didn't look up. "I'd rather just forget about them."

Chrissy said, "I know it's hard, sweetie, but it's like medicine for your feelings. Sometimes medicine tastes bad, but we know we have to take it to get better. It will get easier, I promise." She reached over and squeezed Destiny's hand. "It's kind of like when we have to help the birds exercise their wings after they've been broken. We have to work on the muscles by stretching them gently so they can fly better. The birds don't like it, but it will help them heal faster and get back to their homes quicker."

Destiny stopped coloring and traced a crack in the wood on the coffee table. She was quiet for a moment. "Am I broken?" she asked in a small voice.

Chrissy glanced over at Jake. Her eyes welled with tears for this child who had been through so much. "You were broken. But you are healing now. Jake and I want to help you. Miss Laura wants to help you. This lady, her name is Helen, will help you, too. We all want to see you fly!" She smiled through her tears.

Destiny nodded. She looked at Chrissy and said, "I guess you can be broken where it doesn't show, can't you."

Chrissy nodded and wrapped her arms around Destiny. She didn't trust her voice in the least.

The next day, they drove Destiny to see Helen. Her office was in an old house that had been converted into office space. The living room was now a waiting room with leather couches arranged around a fireplace.

Helen met them at the door. She was a short, middle-aged woman with graying brown hair.

She had reading glasses perched on her head. Her fawn-colored pants coordinated with the geometric printed silk blouse she wore.

Helen took Destiny into what was once a bedroom that had been turned into a treatment room. It was large and had a small table, a couch, a few comfortable chairs, and a toy box. Destiny wandered around, looking at everything. She picked up a doll from the toy box, looked at it, and put it back. She moved a stuffed red cartoon dog to the side and dug around in the bottom of the box. She pulled out a puppet in the form of an owl. She put her hand inside and made the wings move.

Turning to Helen, she said, "Do you know what kind of owl this is?"

Helen shook her head. She was standing by the door, watching Destiny. "No, do you?"

Destiny nodded. She used her free hand to pet the owl's head. "This is a great horned owl. You can tell because of the feathers growing out on its head. They look like horns. We have one at the Rehab Center right now. It got hit by a car last week. It has a broken wing."

"That's so sad, Destiny," Helen said. She picked up a notepad from the table and wrote something. "Is it going to be OK?"

"Oh, yes, we have set its wing and put it in an enclosure to heal. I have been helping to make food for it and I get to watch the physical therapist work with it. After the bones grow back together, I mean."

Helen sat at the table and pulled out a card game. "Come sit with me, Destiny."

Destiny put the owl back in the toy box and came over to the table. Helen had put some round cards on the table that had emoji faces on them. "We're going to play a game called Match the Face. I'll ask you a question, and you pick the face that matches how it makes you feel."

Destiny looked at her warily. "That doesn't sound like a fun game."

"Let's try it before you make up your mind, OK?" Helen said. She adjusted some of the cards. "Here's the first one. How do you feel when you are watching the great horned owl?"

Destiny studied the cards. She picked up the smiling one. "I feel happy because he's getting better every day."

"That's great! How about this one: How do you feel when you set a bird free in the wild?" She watched Destiny's face.

Destiny found the excited emoji and waved it. "That's easy. I'm excited to see them go where they belong. Hey, this game isn't that bad."

Helen nodded and said, "What about when a new bird comes to the center that has been injured?

"I feel very sad and anxious," Destiny said, searching for the right face. "I don't like it when animals are hurting. But I'm glad that we can help them get better."

"How did you feel when you got to go visit Susan and her family," Helen asked. Chrissy had filled Helen in on all of Destiny's background when she set up the appointment.

Destiny chose the face with hearts for eyes. "I felt love," she said. "I miss them every day."

Helen paused. Then she asked, "How about when you visited with your mother?"

Destiny shifted in her seat. Looking at the table, she studied the black circles. She chose the one that had a frowning mouth and mad eyebrows. She showed it to Helen. "I felt angry."

"Tell me about it. What made you feel angry?" Helen said. She sat quietly, letting Destiny probe her feelings.

Destiny fiddled with the black card. "I don't know. I just did. Mothers aren't supposed to let their kids go hungry; you know? They are supposed to feed them and take care of them and help them when they are hurt. Can we play something else?" She put down the emoji card and stood up.

Just then, a chime sounded on Helen's phone. Their therapy time was up. Helen walked with Destiny to the waiting room. "Destiny did a great job today," she told Chrissy. "Same time next week?"

"We'll be here," Chrissy said.

"Before you leave, I have a homework assignment for you," Helen said. She walked back to her room and returned holding a soft blue felt bag with the name of the game embossed on it in white. "I'd like you to play this game at home this week. It's called 'Ready for Anything'. I think it will help Destiny develop strategies for when she has to face uncomfortable situations, like seeing her mother again." She opened the bag and pulled out the directions, a soft green plush die with questions on it and a box of cards. She showed Chrissy and Destiny how to play.

"First, make four piles of the cards. All the blue ones in one pile, the green ones, the yellow ones, and the red ones in separate piles. Take turns choosing a card for an activity or event, then roll the die to see what question to answer about it. For example, if you choose the yellow pile, which is the 'Learn and Play' category, you might get the card that says 'play outside'. When you roll the die, you might get the question 'How will I get ready?' The other person has to answer how they would get ready to play outside. Understand?"

"Got it," Chrissy said. "This looks like a fun game." They put everything back in the bag and headed out to the car.

Chrissy started the car and turned onto the street. She looked in the rear-view mirror and asked, "What do you think of Helen?"

Destiny wished she had her red drawing pencil to rub. She shrugged her shoulders and looked out the side window. "She's alright, I guess. Did you know she has a stuffed great horned owl?"

"That's cool," Chrissy said, returning her focus to the road.

Chapter 32

Summer arrived, and with it came blistering heat. The hustle and bustle of regular routines began to wear on Jake and Chrissy. They were also a little on edge, waiting for a phone call saying that Social Services had found Destiny's mother and she would have to resume her weekly visits with her.

"We need a break," Jake said one night after dinner. Destiny and Chrissy were arguing about who's turn it was to fill the dishwasher.

"No argument here," Chrissy said. "What do you think, Destiny?"

Destiny put the plates she was holding into the sink and turned. "What do you mean?"

"You know, take some time off. Unwind. Spend some time in nature," Jake said. "Let's go camping!"

"I've never been camping," Destiny said.

Jake thumped the counter with his fist. "That settles it. Tomorrow, we take Destiny on her first camping trip. Let's go up to Lake Lawrence. It's beautiful up there, you are going to love it!"

He marched into the garage and started pulling equipment off the shelves. He was making such a racket that Destiny went to see if he had fallen and hurt himself. Jake had spilled the tent stakes all over the garage floor. She went and helped him pick them up. They carried the tent to the Suburban and put it in the back, followed by sleeping bags, a camp stove, fishing poles and chairs.

Early the next morning, they took off, stopping at the grocery store to fill the coolers with drinks and food for the trip. They headed up the same road they had gone up to get the owlets, but rounded the big lake and kept climbing higher into the mountains.

Chrissy and Jake taught Destiny several songs to pass the time. When they arrived at Lake Lawrence, they found a campsite near the water. They pulled everything out of the back of the Suburban and taught Destiny how to put up a tent. It took all three of them to put it up. Jake handed her some tent stakes and a hammer and showed her how to secure the corners.

Grabbing the fishing poles, they went down to the water's edge. Jake pulled out a container of worms he had bought at the store.

Destiny cringed. "What are those for?"

"This is what the fish eat," Jake said. "Here, let me show you how to put the bait on your hook." He took a pole and put the worm on the hook.

Destiny put her hands behind her back and shook her head. "I'm not doing that! Gross!"

Jake laughed. "OK. I'll do the gross part. Now watch. Here's how you cast the line into the water." For the next few minutes, he showed Destiny how to handle to pole. On her first cast, the line didn't go out and she smacked the end of the pole into the water. On her second cast, she managed to catch a willow branch beside her. On the third cast, her line went singing out into the lake and the hook landed with a satisfying plop.

Jake and Chrissy cast their lines and they all sat down in the quiet and watched their bobbers. Destiny looked around and smiled. She loved the smells of the pines and the sound of the birds in the trees. The forest around them was calming. She looked up at the bright blue sky and took a deep breath.

Suddenly, Destiny's fishing line went taut and her bobber disappeared beneath the water. She squealed, "Jake, Chrissy, I caught one! I caught one! What do I do?" Jake rushed to her side and showed her how to set the hook by jerking on it, then helped her reel in the wriggly fish. It was a good-sized trout. At first, Destiny didn't want to touch it because it looked slimy, but Chrissy convinced her that it was no big deal.

Jake managed to pry the hook out of the fish's mouth and let Destiny hold it. Chrissy took her picture, standing with her back to the lake, holding the fish in both hands. The look of pride on her face was priceless. They gently returned the fish to the water and set up her fishing line again. The sun slipped slowly behind the mountains as they sat on the shore, enjoying nature and each other's company.

Chrissy finally said, "Anyone besides me getting hungry?"

Destiny nodded her head and reeled in her line. "I am."

"Me, too! I have some worms left over, if you want them," Jake said, shaking the container at Destiny. She ran back to the campsite, laughing.

Jake and Destiny built a small ring of large stones while Chrissy gathered up the food. Jake built a fire in the ring. This was another first for Destiny. She loved it. The orange and red flames, the crackling sound, the warmth all filled her heart with happiness. She walked down to the shoreline with Jake and watched as he cut three green willow branches and stripped the bark off. Jake took his pocket knife and sharpened one end of each stick. They put hotdogs on their sticks and cooked them in the fire. Nothing had ever tasted so good to Destiny. She ate two hotdogs and was reaching for a third when Chrissy said, "Save room for dessert!"

Destiny put the hotdog back in the package. "What's for dessert?"

Jake said, "We're going to have s'mores!"

"Some more what? I haven't eaten any yet," Destiny said, confused.

Jake and Chrissy laughed. Jake said, "That's the name of the dessert – s'mores because they are so good, you'll want s'more!"

Chrissy went to the food box and pulled out a package of marshmallows. "The first thing is to roast the marshmallows over the coals of the fire. Be careful, it's tricky!" Jake helped her push a squishy white marshmallow onto her stick, then did the same to his. He showed her how to place it just high enough over the coals and keep rotating the stick so they got toasty brown on all sides.

Destiny didn't watch hers closely enough and suddenly it caught on fire. "Oh, no!" she said, pulling her stick out of the fire. Jake quickly blew out the flames, but the marshmallow had turned black. "It's OK. You can still eat it that way, or you can try again." Destiny wanted to try again. This time she didn't take her eyes off of it and the marshmallow turned out a nice golden brown.

Chrissy handed her a square of graham cracker and a piece of a chocolate bar. "Put the marshmallow on there," she instructed. Then Chrissy topped it with another graham cracker square, squeezed it all together and pulled it off the stick. Handing the sandwich to Destiny, she said, "Your first s'more!" Destiny bit into the dessert and chewed.

"Wow," she said with her mouth full, "I love these!" She smiled a crooked smile and said, "Can I have s'more?" Jake and Chrissy laughed. They sat around the campfire and watched the flames flicker. Destiny moved closer to Jake and leaned against his leg. She stared into the fire until her eyes grew heavy.

Finally, they doused the fire and cleaned up the food. After washing their sticky hands and faces in the cold lake water, they went into the tent and climbed into their sleeping bags. Destiny lay awake listening to the sounds of the forest. The wind made a soft swishing sound in the tops of the tall pine trees that eventually lulled her to sleep.

The next day was spent hiking the trails around the lake. That night, as Destiny stretched out in her sleeping bag, she said, "Thank you for bringing me here. I love camping. We should do this every weekend."

They woke up with the birds the next morning and packed everything into the Suburban. Destiny threw her arms around one of the trees and said, "Good-bye, forest. We'll be back!"

Now that it was summer, Destiny went to the Rehab Center with Jake and Chrissy every day. She helped clean enclosures, chop up food, clean equipment, stock shelves, anything and everything that they would let her do. Her favorite was traveling with the ambassador birds to educational events. She assisted the volunteers in setting up drop sheets and perches. She set out tables with brochures and pamphlets.

One day, Sharon, the volunteer who handled the smallest bird on the ambassador team, gave Destiny the microphone when they were at a library event. "You know this speech as well as I do, darlin'. Why don't you tell them about the eastern screech owl?" She winked and smiled.

Destiny nodded seriously and took the mic. Turning to the crowd, she said, "This eastern screech owl came from Alabama."

She looked at Sharon, who nodded and said, "Go on. You've got this!"

Destiny took a deep breath. She gripped the microphone in both hands and started talking. "He is red because the trees where he comes from have red bark. He blends in there. The eastern screech owls that are born around here are mostly grayish-brown because that's the color of our trees. When you look at his face, you will notice that his beak has been broken. It healed crooked, so he can't eat right. His eyes are also messed up, so he can't hunt for himself anymore. We have to take care of him now for the rest of his life." Standing in front of the crowd should have made her nervous, but the little bird made her forget where she was.

The crowd asked her questions. She knew the answers to every single one. Destiny discovered a love of public speaking – as long as it was about the birds. She spent every spare moment bugging the people at the Rehab Center with her questions. Everyone there was patient with her and helped her out. She still asked to be allowed into the Critical Care Room, but not as frequently as before. She was too busy. She also continued to have her weekly therapy sessions with Helen. She was opening up more about her life. Jake and Chrissy began going into some of the sessions with her so they could continue the work at home.

Destiny exhausted the books available at the Rehab Center and at the Preston's home as she learned about raptors. "Can we go to the library?" she asked one day as they were driving home.

Chrissy turned around and looked at her. "Whatcha thinking about, sweetie?"

"I need to learn more about raptors," Destiny said.

Chapter 33

After a week of sunshine and perfect weather, the Preston's and Destiny awoke to storm clouds. They were heavy and low. The temperature dipped enough for Chrissy to grab a sweater before they left for the Rehab Center.

Rain spattered the windshield intermittently on the short drive and they made a dash for the building when they arrived. Even with all the lights on inside, the Center felt dark and gloomy. The wind picked up and there were rumbles of thunder in the distance. The lights flickered all morning and twice they went out completely.

As they made their rounds to the enclosures, Jake and Chrissy noticed that the birds were acting very nervous. Some of them were trying to hide in the corners of their enclosures, others were making more noise than usual and flying erratically. The air had a sickly yellow quality.

Destiny sat at Jake's desk, drawing, while Chrissy sat at her desk making schedules for the staff. "What's that noise?" Destiny asked, lifting her head suddenly.

Chrissy looked up from her paperwork. She turned her head, then jumped from her seat. "Get under my desk and stay there!" she yelled at Destiny. She flung open the door and ran from the room. Destiny ignored her command and ran after her. "Jake! The tornado siren is going off!" Chrissy yelled as she ran through the warehouse. When Chrissy opened the door to the back of the property, the wind ripped the door from her hand and it banged into the wall. The trees were whipping around like they were alive.

Chrissy turned and grabbed several carriers and took off for the flight enclosures. Destiny read her mind and grabbed some, too. Destiny took her carriers to the hospital enclosures closest to the building. She picked up some gloves. She had watched the staff catch birds enough to know how to do it safely. She managed to capture one of the Swainson's hawks that were fluttering around its enclosure, trying to escape. She quickly put it into a carrier. She returned to the enclosure and caught another one. Ruth joined her and between the two of them, they managed to catch all the hospital birds just as the rain began to come down in torrents. They picked up the carriers and moved quickly to the building.

With lightning flashing and thunder crashing around them, they grabbed some more carriers and ran towards the larger flight enclosures. Chrissy and Jake were there with others from the staff. Most of the birds were safely in the carriers, but one of the great horned owls that were rehabilitating kept careening around, just out of reach. It was getting harder and harder to see as the rain and wind whipped around them. Suddenly the wind stopped. There was a sound like someone sucking on a straw. Everyone froze.

Jake yelled, "Leave him! Everyone, run for the building!" Jake grabbed Destiny's arm with one hand and a carrier in the other. Chrissy and the staff grabbed the rest of the carriers and they all ran towards the door. Destiny stumbled and would have fallen in the mud if Jake hadn't been holding on to her. They ran inside, put the crates down, shut the door and ran for the office. Inside the office, everyone dove under desks or huddled against the walls.

The wind came back with a rush. This time it sounded like a cross between a scream and a freight train. Under Jake's big desk, Destiny pulled her knees to her chest. She was shaking from cold and fear. Chrissy sat on one side of her and Jake sat on the other. Destiny covered her ears with her hands. Jake and Chrissy wrapped their arms around her and each other. They all closed their eyes as the building shook. It sounded like someone was pouring a bucket of nails onto the roof.

Then it was over. The wind died down, the hail stopped, the air became quiet. There was a gentle patter of rain on the roof. In the pitch black of the office, everyone slowly stood up. "Are you all OK?" Jake asked, his voice shaking. He reached back under the desk and found the emergency flashlight still plugged into the outlet. He flicked it on and looked around the room. Quiet sobs and lots of hugs were shared as they checked each other for injuries. Everyone seemed OK, aside from a few bumps and bruises.

Bracing themselves for what they would find on the other side of the door, Jake turned the knob and pulled it open. There was a faint glow coming down the hallway from the warehouse, but the rest of the building remained as dark as an underground cavern. Cell phones came out and people used their flashlight feature to find their way around. As a group, they walked down the hall to the large warehouse. A corner of the roof was peeled back; daylight and rain were coming in through the opening. They could hear the birds rustling around in the carriers where they had set them down.

Jake walked slowly past them to the door to the outdoor enclosures. Grimly, he gripped the handle and pulled. Everyone gasped at what they saw. Where once had been neat, orderly rows of cages was now a pile of broken boards. It reminded Destiny of the time she had accidentally spilled a box of toothpicks on the kitchen counter. Some walls were intact and others looked like broken teeth. Pieces of chicken wire were wrapped around, under, and over the mess. It smelled like a freshly tilled garden.

"Oh, no!" Chrissy cried, holding her hand to her mouth. They all picked their way out into the middle of the mess. No one even felt the rain that was gently falling. The hospital enclosures were completely gone. The flight enclosures were completely unrecognizable. "We have to find the great horned owl," she said.

Slowly and carefully, hoping with all their hearts, the staff and volunteers began to clear away the broken boards. They moved tree branches that had crushed walls. They stacked boards that were still useable. Every time they lifted a piece of debris, they prayed they'd find the bird alive. Destiny and Chrissy worked together to lift a large branch when something under it moved. Kneeling in the mud they cleared away fallen leaves. Staring back at them with its big brown eyes was the owl. Its feathers were a soggy mess. It looked at them and hissed. It tried to move away from them, but one of its wings was twisted in an unnatural way.

"We found the owl!" Chrissy said. Everyone dropped what they were doing and rushed to see. Eager hands reached down and lifted the large branch off the bird. Ignoring the clacking beak and angry sounds, Chrissy gently picked it up out of the mud and, cradling it against her chest, carried it inside. Destiny followed her with the flashlight. Jake joined them and they took the owl to the Critical Care Room.

Destiny stopped in the doorway. "Can I help?" she asked. She looked around the space and in the low light saw stainless steel countertops, white cabinets, and long tables. There were small metal cages against one wall with heat lamps above them.

Jake and Chrissy looked up briefly from the table where they had lain the owl on its back. "Yes, Destiny, we need you. Grab that old blue towel and come cover the owl's eyes. It will calm him down if he can't see us. You can hold the flashlight."

Destiny picked up the towel and crossed the room. She gently folded the towel across the muddy bird's head and watched Chrissy and Jake work. She held the flashlight high and pointed it down onto the bird.

Jake palpated each of the bones in the bird's bent wing. "There are multiple fractures here," he said. He and Chrissy cleaned off the mud as best they could and splinted the wing with popsicle sticks, wrapping it in gauze and tape to stabilize it. "That will have to do for now," he said.

Placing the bird in one of the metal cages, the three left the Critical Care Room. They headed back outside to help staff clear the debris and see what could be saved. The sun was trying to break through the clouds, and Destiny had to squint for a minute. The area behind the main building was a wreck. None of the outdoor enclosures had survived the tornado. One of the giant old trees near the edge of the property had been uprooted. There was a giant crater where it used to stand. In the distance, she could hear sirens.

Now that the danger had passed, Destiny's knees began shaking. She found a pile of boards that one of the volunteers had stacked and sat down on it. She wrapped her arms around her knees and sat there rocking. Chrissy noticed her and came over. She sat down next to Destiny and put her arms around her. They didn't speak, but instead, just rocked back and forth together.

Finally, Destiny broke the silence. "Why," she said.

"I don't know," Chrissy said. "Things just happen. The good news is that no one here got hurt. This is just stuff. Stuff can be replaced. People can't. The animals are all OK, and the owl's injuries will heal."

"No, I mean why wouldn't he let us help him?" Destiny asked, looking up at Chrissy. "If he hadn't been so stubborn and flew around so crazy, he wouldn't have gotten hurt."

Chrissy tucked a strand of hair behind Destiny's ear. "He was scared, Destiny. When animals – and people, too – get scared, they don't use their brains. They don't think logically. They think that everyone and everything is out to get them, out to hurt them. Their instincts take over and all they can think about is getting away from whatever they think the danger is."

"So, he panicked?" Destiny said. "When I get really mad or scared, I just want to run away. I don't stop to think that someone is trying to help me."

"That's called your fight or flight instinct," Chrissy explained. "Part of your brain is wired to protect you by getting you out of what it thinks is a dangerous situation. It isn't logical, it's pure action."

Chrissy stood up and held out her hand. "Let's see if we can help get some temporary enclosures put together. Those poor birds can't stay cramped up in the carriers all night." Destiny stood and let Chrissy put her arm around her shoulders as they walked together across the uneven ground.

Chapter 34

When they arrived home that night, they were relieved to find that their home had escaped the tornado's path. The power was still off, so they scrounged in the kitchen for dinner. They ended up making peanut butter and jelly sandwiches.

Chrissy said, "It's been a long day. Everybody to bed." She led Destiny upstairs and helped her climb under the covers.

"Please stay with me," Destiny said in a small voice. Once again, Chrissy climbed onto the bed and lay her head next to Destiny's. They fell asleep almost instantly, they were so exhausted. When Jake came upstairs, he peeked in on them and smiled. He found an extra blanket in the hall closet and covered Chrissy with it.

The next day, the staff gathered at the Rehab Center for a meeting. The power was still off, so they stood in the parking lot. Jake stood on the tailgate of a truck and began the meeting by saying, "We can look at this situation in one of two ways. A tragedy, or an opportunity. Yes, it sucks that our enclosures were destroyed, but we now have an opportunity to make this facility even better than it was before."

As he was speaking, a large white van with a local news station logo on the side pulled into the parking lot. The crowd turned to look. Four men jumped out and joined the crowd. One was carrying a large camera on his shoulder. Another had a microphone and was wearing a blue polo shirt with the news logo on it. The staff made room for them and Jake continued talking.

"As I was saying, we got lucky. Now we have the chance to make some changes to make things even better for our birds. Let's go make sure the raptors are fed and as comfortable as we can for now. I want all of you to think about ideas for what the new Rehab Center will look like." He hopped down from the truck. The staff went inside quickly while Jake and Chrissy introduced themselves to the news reporter.

"Welcome to the Raptor Rehabilitation Center, or what's left of it," he said. "I'm Jake Preston, and this is my wife, Chrissy. We run the operations here. How can I help you?"

The man with the microphone said, "I'm David O'Donnell from Channel 8 Action News. Would you mind doing an interview with us about the damage you sustained?"

Jake said, "Not at all. Maybe the exposure will get us some donations of materials to rebuild."

After the interview, Jake and Chrissy took the news crew on a tour of the facility. They showed them the makeshift enclosures and talked about how they had to be careful about which birds they placed together in the cramped quarters.

Jake explained, "Some birds become very aggressive about their territory and will fight other birds. Right now, they are all stressed out and could end up injuring themselves. We need to rebuild as soon as possible so they can heal and be released into the wild. Our educational birds are more used to small spaces because they travel with us, but they need more room, too. This is how diseases spread."

He walked the crew out to their van and then joined Chrissy and Destiny in the office.

"Are you going to be on TV?" Destiny asked. "You could be famous!"

Jake laughed and said, "I probably won't become famous over this, but I do hope that this will spread the word about the supplies we need to rebuild. That David guy said to watch the 7 o'clock news tonight. I hope the power is back on by then."

That night the power was back on and Jake, Chrissy, and Destiny made sure that they were sitting in front of the TV at exactly 7. The leading story was the tornado and they watched helicopter footage of the path it had taken.

Destiny stiffened and let out a gasp. She pointed at the TV. "That's my old school!" Part of the roof was caved in and the playground equipment was a tangled mess. Jake quickly reached for the remote, but he wasn't fast enough. The next shot was a row of houses on a dead-end street. Destiny gripped Chrissy's arm. "That's my old neighborhood!" Every single house on the street was a pile of debris. Not a single one was left standing. "There's my house! There's nothing left!" She started crying.

Jake clicked the TV off. There were no words to say, so they sat and held Destiny and cried with her. Destiny was inconsolable. When Destiny had cried herself out, Chrissy led her upstairs and helped her get ready for bed. Chrissy lay down on Destiny's bed and stayed with her until she fell asleep.

Jake put in a call to Helen's office but was unable to reach her. He left a message detailing the latest developments and asked her to call back as soon as she was able.

After that night, Destiny never mentioned what she had seen on TV. She never asked about her mom. When Chrissy or Jake brought it up, Destiny would quickly change the subject. Instead, she poured herself into drawing new designs for the flight enclosures and helping with rebuilding the Center.

When Helen called back, she said, "It's normal for some children who experience trauma to try to shut it out instead of dealing with their feelings."

Chrissy asked her, "Isn't that going to cause problems down the road for Destiny?" She was pacing between the kitchen and living room.

"She will have to deal with it eventually," Helen said. "But this is a survival mechanism that she has perfected. She's a survivor. This is her, coping with things she doesn't understand. Give her time. We'll work on it at her next visit."

Over dinner one night, Chrissy couldn't help herself. She asked Destiny, "How are you doing?"

"I'm fine, why?" Destiny asked, wrinkling her nose.

"I mean how are you feeling about what happened with the tornado, with your house," Chrissy said. She twirled some pasta on her fork.

Destiny shrugged her shoulders and played with the peas on her dinner plate.

"Are you worried about your mom?" Jake asked. His eyes never left Destiny's face.

"She never worried about me, so why should I be worried about her?" Destiny said, standing up. Her chair scraped loudly against the floor. "Can I be excused?" Her voice was calm, but her eyes weren't.

Jake nodded. "Sure, Champ." He looked at Chrissy with concern.

Destiny went upstairs to her bedroom. She rummaged around in her dresser until she found her old sweatshirt. She put it on over her head, pulled the hood down around her face, and climbed onto the bed. She tucked her hands into the pocket and leaned against the headboard. She squeezed her eyes closed and tried not to think, but the memories leaked out just as fast as the tears.

Chapter 35

The next day was a red-letter day for the Rehab Center. Because of the coverage by the news station, donations poured in and the phone rang off the hook with people volunteering to come and help them rebuild. Unfortunately, the emergency line kept ringing as well, with more injured birds from the storm.

The whole staff was standing outside the main door when the lumber truck showed up that morning. You would have thought that they had won the lottery by the noise they made. Destiny was the loudest of all. Wood had become scarce since the tornado. Everyone was trying to rebuild their homes and their lives. One of the lumber yards in town was owned by the spouse of a staff member, and Jake had convinced them to save a load for the Rehab Center.

Volunteers had come the day before and dug the holes that would hold the tall posts for the flight enclosures. Bags of quick setting cement sat next to them, ready to secure the posts. They unloaded the eight-foot boards and piled them inside the warehouse. The round wooden posts went in the next pile. The smell of fresh-cut lumber was intoxicating. The first project was going to be the flight enclosure for their largest raptors.

Destiny was ecstatic. When Jake had seen her drawings for the build, he had immediately taken them and had an architect turn them into blueprints. She was running between the piles and the trucks and getting in everyone's way. Chrissy called her over, "Let's go check in on the great horned owl in the Critical Care Room." Destiny only looked over her shoulder once as she followed Chrissy inside.

The owl was slowly recovering. The large bone at the top of the wing was broken in two places. One of the pieces had slipped out of place and was sticking up out of the skin. It was the same place that it had been broken when the bird had first been brought to the center after being hit by a car.

Destiny stood in front of the stainless-steel enclosure watching the owl. It had puffed up its feathers, tucked its head down, and was hissing at her. Every once in a while, it would thrust its head forward and clack its beak at her.

"Why is he trying to bite us?" Destiny asked, "We're trying to help him."

Chrissy said, "It is in pain and doesn't understand it. The owl thinks that we are causing the discomfort and is lashing out. Remember, this is a wild animal and isn't used to being around humans. We try to keep our distance from all our wild birds as much as possible so they don't get used to us. We want them to return to the wild and stay away from people." She shook her head. "This one was just about ready to be released, too."

Destiny looked sadly at the bird. It had large yellow eyes that never seemed to blink in a wide brown face. "It's OK," she said in her most soothing voice. "We won't hurt you." All she got in return was a clacking of the beak and a loud hiss.

Jake came into the room. Chrissy said, "What do you think, Jake? Its wing is pretty bad. I don't think we have the equipment to do this complex of a break, especially one that was almost healed when it got broken again."

Scratching his head, Jake said, "It needs to go up to the university. They are better equipped to help this kind of thing." Rocky Mountain

University, with one of the best veterinary schools in the country, was just across town from the Raptor Rehabilitation Center. Over the years, Jake and Chrissy had established a great working relationship with them and often conferred cases with them.

"I'll call them right now," Chrissy said, reaching for her phone.

Jake motioned to Destiny to follow him. "Come see what's going on out back," he said. They went through the back door and into a hive of activity. There were large poles sticking straight up out of the ground like giant toothpicks. People were hauling five-gallon buckets of water and others were shaking bags of dry cement into the holes. Destiny stood there with her mouth open, staring. All the debris had been hauled away. The toppled tree had been sawn into chunks and removed. The ground had been raked. It looked like a completely different place. Destiny reached for Jake's hand and gave it a squeeze. He looked down at her beaming face and smiled.

Chrissy came up behind them. "The university said they'd take the owl, but we have to transport it ourselves. Destiny, are you up for a little drive?"

Letting go of Jake's hand, she turned and said, "Let's go!" She led the way back to the Critical Care Room.

Chrissy grabbed a large towel and covered the carrier. "Why do you always cover the carriers?" Destiny asked.

"To keep out the light and so the bird can't see us. It needs to rest. You saw how it reacted when we went near it. We don't want to add to the stress its already feeling. That's also why we don't let very many people come into the Critical Care Room. The birds frighten easily and might hurt themselves worse if they are trying to get away from us."

Destiny suddenly had a flashback of the time she had run away from Susan's house. She had run to the park and sat in that little fort. Now it reminded her of a bird enclosure. She could still see Miss Laura cramming herself into that tiny space with her. She remembered how frightened and angry she had been, and how Miss Laura had just sat there, calmly, waiting for Destiny to stop being scared. Destiny felt like she understood the owl better than anyone.

They put the carrier in the back of the Suburban and drove over to the veterinary hospital on the university campus. On the way there, they'd had to detour around streets covered with debris and wait for big dump trucks helping with the cleanup. They pulled into the parking lot and stopped in front of the large stone building. The front doors opened and a man in green scrubs came out with a stainless-steel table on wheels. Chrissy and Destiny jumped out and opened the back doors to the Suburban. The man helped them put the owl's cage onto the table.

"Good-bye, my friend," Destiny whispered to the owl while Chrissy and the doctor spoke. The doctor turned the table around and headed back inside the building.

"That's it?" Destiny said. "You aren't even going to go in with the owl?" She watched the doors close behind the doctor.

"I spoke with Dr. Paul on the phone before we came. He knows everything we've done. Relax, Destiny. He's the best in the business. Our owl is in good hands," Chrissy said, patting Destiny on the back.

Chapter 36

Three days later, the back of the Rehab center was a completely different place. It still smelled like fresh lumber, but no broken boards were lying around, or tree limbs and leaves littering the ground. The birds were already using the new enclosures, but the staff decided that they needed to have a ribbon-cutting ceremony.

All morning, the staff worked in the warehouse. They moved boxes and swept the floor. They created a large space in the middle and set up folding tables. Destiny was given rolls of crepe paper and told to decorate to her heart's content. She swagged the paper around the perimeter of the room and the edges of the table. She used blue, green, pink, and yellow streamers. Soon, the guests began arriving, along with the cake and a local high school band. Jake had also invited the news crew back. They came in with their camera gear and started unpacking.

Destiny went into the office and changed into her new party dress. It was light blue and had daisies sewn onto the skirt. Chrissy brushed Destiny's hair and put a blue and white bow in it. She thought back to when she'd first met Destiny. She had been dirty, unkempt and scrawny. It was hard to recognize this glowing happy girl as the same child.

Jake put a suit coat over his t-shirt and ran a comb through his black hair. Chrissy changed into a white sundress with a blue sash. Together, they went out to the warehouse.

As soon as they walked around the corner, a cheer broke out. Jake held up his hands and shook his head. "Hey! All this was possible because of you guys, not us," he said. "Not that I don't enjoy the limelight, but today is about the volunteers who put their blood, sweat, and tears into making this place what it is. We couldn't have done it without you!" The crowd broke into applause. "Let's go out back and get this party started!" He turned around and went to the back door.

They had stretched a blue ribbon across the compound between two of the enclosures. When everyone had found a spot and had quieted down, Jake pulled out some note cards and cleared his throat. "May 30, a day that we will never forget. A day that could have ended in tragedy and loss of life, became a blessing in disguise. We turned it into an opportunity to make this place an even better place for birds of prey to heal and recover. Thank you all for your help in making this a reality." He turned to Chrissy, who picked up three pairs of scissors that were lying nearby. She handed a pair to Destiny and one to Jake.

The crowd counted, "One, two, three!" The ribbon fell into three parts. The crowd cheered while Destiny hugged Chrissy, then turned and hugged Jake.

"Let's go eat some cake," Jake said and ushered everyone back inside the warehouse. The band played some cover songs from the 80s and there was lots of laughter.

The next day was Destiny's weekly appointment with Helen. Destiny couldn't wait to tell her all about the party. She walked into the therapy room and saw a box of brand-new colored pencils and some blank paper lying on the table. "Are we going to do an art project?" she asked.

Helen nodded and smiled. "Yes! I heard that you are a budding artist and thought you might enjoy it."

"Cool!" Destiny said. "Can I draw a picture of the party we had yesterday?"

"Only if you promise to talk to me about it while you draw it," Helen said. "I'm sorry I missed it. Sounds like it was a lot of fun."

Destiny wasted no time spilling the colored pencils onto the table and grabbing a piece of paper. "It was the best. I got to decorate the whole warehouse. It was beautiful. I put streamers everywhere. I only wish I could have put up balloons, but Jake wouldn't let me. He said they would scare the birds if they popped. I guess he's right. They would have looked pretty, though."

Helen sat at the table across from Destiny and watched as the scene developed on the page. She let Destiny relax and talk about the party without interruption. Soon, the picture was finished. Destiny held it up for Helen to see. "What do you think?" she asked.

Helen reached for the page. "I think this is magnificent work. I love all the details you included. It almost comes alive. You did a wonderful job decorating." She paused. "Would you draw another picture for me?" she asked.

Destiny reached for another sheet of paper. "Sure. What do you want me to draw? Do you want to see what the ribbon-cutting ceremony was like?" She picked up a pencil.

"I want you to draw a picture of your mother," Helen said. She kept her voice even and calm.

Destiny recoiled and dropped the pencil as if it were on fire. She sat back in her chair and looked at Helen with big eyes. "I don't want to."

"Please. I've never seen her and I want you to show me what she looks like to you." She picked up the pencil that Destiny had dropped and held it out.

"Forget it. I'd rather draw a picture of the golden eagle we have," Destiny shook her head and pursed her lips. She sat on her hands.

Helen tried one more time. "Draw a picture of you and your mother. What do you remember about her?"

Destiny leaned forward and sighed. "Fine. You're never going to let this go until I do, are you?"

Helen said, "Thank you. This means a lot to me."

Destiny reached for the pencils and thought for a moment. Then she began to draw. She picked up a light gray pencil and leaned close to the page. She drew tiny straight lines carefully. Then she picked up a dark purple one and made giant sweeping swirls across the entire page. More colors, mostly dark, were chosen. It didn't take long for her to become absorbed in the picture. As she drew with the black pencil, her grip grew tighter and tighter. The lines became bolder and more jagged. She scrubbed the paper so hard that she tore a hole in it. Her breathing was shallow and her eyes dilated.

A small sound came from Destiny's throat and her breathing became jagged like her lines. Finally, she took the pencil in both hands and snapped it in two. Then she shoved the paper across the table and said, "There! Are you happy now?" Her cheeks were wet and her face was red. She swiped the back of her hand across her eyes and tried to stick her hands in her pocket, only to realize that she wasn't wearing her beloved sweatshirt. Instead, she rolled them under the edge of her shirt.

Helen picked up the picture gently and studied it. In the middle of the page, barely visible under all the black and purple swirls, was a small, gray mattress. Sitting on it cross-legged was a small child, drawn in pale pink. The dark swirls surrounding the mattress and girl took up the whole rest of the page, forming the shape of a woman. The woman's eyes were red. She was pointing a black fingernail at the child. The woman's mouth was wide open. The pain, fear, and misery Destiny had portrayed almost dripped off the paper.

Softly, Helen said, "Tell me about the picture." She set in back on the table.

Destiny slowly leaned forward and picked up the paper. "It's not finished yet," she said. Then she proceeded to crumple the paper into a ball. Then she flattened it once again. "There," she said. She leaned back again, tucking her hands under the hem of her shirt, and staring at the picture.

Helen smoothed the page with her hands. "Why did you crumple it up?"

Destiny shrugged. "You wanted to know what my mother is like. Now you know."

Helen nodded. She studied the figures. She noticed a detail that she had overlooked on her first glance. A tiny bit of red amidst all the black. She picked up the drawing and looked closer. It was a very small heart on the woman's chest. "Let's turn this picture into a story," she said. "I'll start. Once upon a time, there was a woman and her child. Now it's your turn."

"They lived in an old broken house. The end," Destiny said, standing up. She walked across the room to the toy box. She kept her back to Helen and began aimlessly picking up toys.

"Not the end," Helen said. "That was the beginning. What is the little girl on the bed thinking?" She stayed at the table, giving Destiny some space.

Destiny shrugged her shoulders and continued to play with the toys. She found a stuffed cat in the box and pulled it out. She sat cross-legged on the floor and put it in her lap. She stroked the cat's head.

"Then what is the mother saying to the little girl?" Helen pushed.

Destiny leaned over the cat and said, "Don't listen to her, Fur Ball. Maybe she'll go back inside and leave us alone."

"The little girl on the bed looks small and lonely, Destiny. Is that how you feel?"

Destiny turned around and looked at Helen. "Can we be done with this? I drew your stupid picture. I don't want to talk about it anymore." She was hugging the cat to her chest. Her face was calm, but her pupils were dilated and her nostrils flared.

Helen recognized the cornered look on Destiny's face. She didn't want to break the fragile trust they had built. So, she nodded her head and smiled. Standing up, she crossed the room to sit on the floor next to

Destiny. "Tell me about the cat."

Destiny looked down at the stuffed animal. "I don't have a cat."

"I heard you call the cat Fur Ball."

"Yeah, Fur Ball is a stray cat. He lived in my neighborhood. He was such a mooch. When I got home at night, I sat on the back steps of my house. He came over and kept me company. He'd eat practically anything I gave him. He really liked cheese. You know those yellow sticks they give you at school for breakfast? Those were his favorites. Then he curled up in my lap and purred. I could feel him vibrating against my legs. He let me pet him." Destiny's eyes were soft. She stroked the stuffed animal in her lap as she talked. Her shoulders relaxed and her breathing returned to normal.

The timer on Helen's phone went off. Destiny stood up and returned the toy to the toy box. Helen got up and walked her to the door. After Destiny left, Helen picked up the paper from the table and gently touched the little girl in the middle of the chaos. *Why?* she asked herself. *Just why?*

Chapter 37

Laura made regular visits to see Destiny, so it wasn't out of the ordinary for her to show up at the Rehab Center on occasion. What was out of the ordinary on this visit was the ashen look on her face.

When she stepped into the office, she shut the door and said, "Where's Destiny?"

Jake and Chrissy looked at each other in alarm. "What's wrong? What's going on?" Chrissy asked, standing quickly.

"Destiny is helping in the Mouse Room. Let me go get her," Jake said, walking to the door.

Laura grabbed his arm and said, "No. Don't get her yet. We need to talk first." Jake and Chrissy sat back down, but Laura paced the tiny room. Jake and Chrissy looked wide-eyed at each other.

"I don't know how to tell you this," Laura started. She wouldn't look at them.

"Are you taking Destiny away from us?" Chrissy cried. She put her hands over her face. Jake scooted his chair over to her and put his arms around her.

Laura shook her head and put her hand on Chrissy's shoulder. "No, I'm not taking Destiny away from you. Far from it. I've never had this happen before. I just got a call from the sheriff's office. They located Destiny's mother. She's dead."

The Prestons sat in shocked silence. Chrissy began to cry and so did Laura. Chrissy stood and the two women held each other. Jake stood and put his arms around both of them. They cried for Destiny, for whom the bad breaks never seemed to end. They cried for her mother, who couldn't seem to get her life together, and now she never would. They cried because there was no easy way to tell a child that her parent was now gone. Not only had she been neglected, abused, and abandoned, she was now an orphan. What was going to happen to her?

"What are we going to do? What happens now?" Chrissy asked between sobs. "How are we going to tell Destiny? I don't know how she is going to react to this."

Laura said, "Maybe we should contact her therapist and ask her how to handle this." She took the Kleenex Jake offered and wiped her eyes.

Jake and Chrissy nodded.

"We don't know much about the circumstances, so we should hold off telling her until we know more," Laura added. Suddenly she looked ten years older.

With a plan in place, they hugged each other one more time. Chrissy walked out to the front of the building with Laura. She said good-bye and went to sit in the Suburban to call Helen. There was no way that she wanted Destiny to overhear the conversation.

The next few days were tough for Chrissy and Jake. They had to act like it was business as usual, but every time they looked at Destiny, the sadness they felt was almost overwhelming.

Laura called and said, "I spoke with the sheriff's department again. They told me that they had found Destiny's mother under a tree in a park. They suspect it was an overdose."

Chrissy said, "Thank you for the update. Destiny's regular appointment with Helen is today. I'll call her and let her know of these developments." She bit her lip and dialed Helen's number.

At Helen's office, they sat nervously in the waiting room. Destiny kept looking at Chrissy. "Why are you shaking your leg so much? Do you need to use the bathroom?"

Chrissy put her hand on her leg and tried to smile. "Sorry. No, I don't need to use the bathroom. I was just thinking about something." Destiny seemed to buy her lame excuse and she walked over to look out the window.

Helen came into the waiting room and greeted them. "Hello! I think that today I'd like all three of you to join the session. Is that OK?" she asked, turning to Destiny.

Destiny shrugged her shoulders. "Sure, I guess."

As they walked into the therapy room. Helen gestured to the grouping of chairs and couches. "Let's sit over here, it's more comfortable." Jake and Chrissy sat on the couch with Destiny between them. Helen chose a chair across from them.

Helen started the session by saying, "Destiny, we have something to tell you. There is some bad news."

Destiny stiffened. She turned her head to look at Jake, and then at Chrissy. Jake's lips were pressed tightly together, and tears were already streaming down Chrissy's cheeks. Her face went pale and she clenched her fists. "I'm going to another foster home, aren't I? I did something wrong, didn't I. You don't want me anymore."

Speaking slowly, Helen said, "No, no, Destiny. You are staying with Jake and Chrissy. You are not going to another foster home. This is about your mother. She died, Destiny." Helen paused, watching Destiny carefully. Looking for her reaction. Jake and Chrissy held their breath and watched, too. Destiny just sat there. No reaction.

"We are here for you, Destiny," Helen said. "I know this is a shock. Just know that we are here for you. This isn't something easy to deal with."

Destiny didn't say a word. She slid off the couch and crawled over to the box of toys. She dug around until she found the stuffed cat. She held the toy in her arms and petted its head, rocking back and forth. The adults sat in silence and watched. Finally, Chrissy couldn't stand it anymore. She went over and knelt beside Destiny and put her arms around her shoulders. Jake came and did the same thing on the other side of her. Destiny sat rigidly, still as a statue. Then she stood up, shaking off the affection. "What's the big deal?" she said.

Helen said, "It's OK to feel sad that she died. Do you have any questions about it?"

"No," Destiny said. She turned her back on everyone.

Destiny felt numb. Her mother was dead. So what? It wasn't like her mother had cared for her or had wanted her. In her mind, her mother was gone anyway. Why was Chrissy crying about it? It was no big deal, right?

She tried to block out the talking around her. Why couldn't they just drop it? She didn't want to think about it. She focused her attention on the little stuffed cat she had picked up. It looked just like Fur Ball.

Her mind went back to sitting on the back steps of the run-down house, holding the cat in her lap, feeling its soft fur, hearing its contented purring. She could still feel the vibration against her legs. Such a soothing sound.

She tried to take a deep breath. It wouldn't come. She walked over to the door, opened it, and ran out of the room. She crossed the waiting room and wrenched open the door. She ran blindly down the sidewalk. She ran as if someone was chasing her. As if her mother was chasing her, trying to get her to go back to her pitiful room, to sit against that wall on that dirty mattress. Small whimpering noises started to escape her lips.

She turned corners, ran down streets, through alleys, across lawns, never seeing any of it. She tripped on an exposed tree root and fell flat on her stomach. She stood and ran on, not feeling the blood trickling from her scraped knees. To her, the world had become dark and scary.

Her blood rushed in her ears; tears blurred her vision. On she ran. She began gasping for air, but still she ran. She ran until her legs gave out. She collapsed against a fence, pulled her legs to her chest and closed her eyes.

Slowly, the world came back into focus. Her heart started to beat normally; her breathing calmed down. Sweat glistened on her face. She opened her eyes and looked around her. She didn't recognize where she was. She looked down and saw the stuffed cat lying next to her. She picked it up and hugged it to her chest.

She felt tired. Tired from running, yes, but it was more than that. She leaned back against the fence, closed her eyes, and cried. Finally, she fell into an exhausted sleep.

Blinding lights on her face woke her up. Headlights were coming towards her. She put up her arm to shield her eyes. The car stopped. The lights went out and it was dark all around her. Destiny rubbed her eyes. She didn't know where she was or what she had done. A car door opened and closed. Feet crunched on gravel. A shadowy figure came towards her and crouched down next to her.

"Well, hello!" the man said in a deep voice.

Destiny just stared at him; her eyes wide. He was a big man with a curly brown beard. His eyes were large and dark. He was smiling at her.

"What's your name?" he asked. "How did you get here? Are you lost?"

Destiny nodded, clutching the stuffed animal and looking like a street urchin with her messy hair, dirty face and bloody knees.

"My name is Rob," the man said. "This is my house. Let's see if we can get you home, OK?" Rob reached down to take her hand. Destiny hesitated, then put her hand in his and let him help her up. They walked up the gravel driveway to the house. He opened the door and led Destiny inside.

"Honey, look what I found by the garage," he said, taking Destiny into the brightly lit kitchen.

A short, heavy-set woman at the stove turned and looked. Dropping her spoon back into the pot, she said, "Oh, my! Who is this?"

Rob looked at Destiny and said, "This is my wife, Janice. She is the best cook in the city. Are you hungry?"

Destiny nodded.

Janice pulled out a kitchen chair. "Sit here and I'll get you something to eat. What's your name, dear?"

"Destiny," came the quiet answer.

"Where are you from?" Janice asked. Destiny shrugged, hugging her cat tightly. Janice brought her some bread and butter. "Dinner's almost ready. Why don't you eat this while you wait?"

Rob left the room. Destiny could hear his deep voice as he talked on the phone. Soon he returned and sat at the table. He smiled at Destiny. "I just got off the phone with the police. Your family has been searching for you all day. An officer will be here in a little while to take you home. Let's eat before they get here, OK?"

Janice brought Destiny a plate filled with fried chicken, mashed potatoes and gravy and green beans. She brought another one for Rob and herself. They sat down at the table and tried to get her to talk while they ate. She kept her eyes on her plate and only gave them shrugs and one-word answers.

Just as they were finishing their meal, the doorbell rang. Rob went to answer it and brought a police officer into the kitchen. "Destiny, this is Officer Max. He is here to take you home."

Rob and Janice followed them out to the black patrol car. Destiny turned to them and said, "Thanks for the food." Janice gave her a hug and Rob patted her shoulder.

"Glad you are safe. Take care of yourself," Rob said.

Destiny had never seen the inside of a police car before. She sat in the back on a seat of hard, molded black plastic. Between the front and rear seats was a sheet of clear plastic with holes in it. The police radio would beep and people talked non-stop. Destiny saw a computer mounted next to the driver's seat.

When they pulled up in front of the Preston's house, Jake and Chrissy ran over to the car. Behind them were Helen and Laura. She also saw a crowd of people standing on the lawn. She recognized most of them from the Rehab Center.

When the officer opened the door for her, Chrissy hugged her tight and said, "Thank God, you're OK. We were so worried about you!" Destiny hugged her back, breathing in the scent of her perfume.

"Hey, give me a turn," Jake said. Chrissy stepped back, wiping her eyes. Jake's muscled arms pulled Destiny close. He kissed the top of her head and said, "I love you, Destiny. I'm so glad you are home." She buried her face against his shirt and leaned against him.

Destiny was passed from person to person. Destiny ducked her head and endured the attention. She had never had anyone make this big of a fuss over her. Finally, Jake and Chrissy told everyone good night and took Destiny inside.

Upstairs, they both tucked her into bed. As badly as they wanted to talk about where she had been and why she had run, they decided to wait until morning. They kissed her cheeks, her forehead, and the top of her head. "We are so glad you are home, Destiny. We were scared that we would never find you," Chrissy said.

Destiny didn't know what to say to that. So, she didn't say anything at all. She simply closed her eyes. Jake and Chrissy took the hint and left her. They turned off the light but left the door open. They went to their room and got ready for bed. Soon, the house was still and dark. Neither Jake nor Chrissy could sleep, though. In spite of being exhausted, they lay awake and stared at the ceiling.

A few hours later, the sound of screaming jolted them from their bed. They ran to Destiny's room and found her still asleep, but thrashing her arms and crying out. "Destiny, wake up," Jake said. He picked her up and held her in his arms. Chrissy put her hands on either side of Destiny's face.

"Wake, up, Destiny. You are having a bad dream. It's OK. You are safe. We are here," she said. Destiny's eyes were wide and unseeing. Slowly she relaxed and calmed down. She blinked her eyes and looked around.

"What happened," she asked hoarsely. Her chest was heaving and she was drenched in sweat. She looked up at Jake. She squirmed herself around in Jake's arms and threw her arms around his neck. She buried her face into his neck and hung on, shivering. He held her tightly to him, rocking slightly until she stopped shaking. Chrissy sat next to them, rubbing Destiny's back. Jake held her the rest of the night, leaning back against the headboard, never letting go.

Chapter 38

The funeral was a quiet one, held in the cemetery. The only people in attendance were Jake, Chrissy, Destiny, Laura, Helen, and some of the staff of the Rehab Center. Destiny held the stuffed cat that had become her constant companion. They gathered at the gravesite to say their good-byes to a woman that none of them knew.

Helen had helped Destiny to write a short poem for her mother. She read it quickly:

"Good-by, Mother

Be with the angels.

May you rest in peace."

Then, Chrissy handed her a white rose and she placed in on the simple wooden casket. A pastor was there to say a few words to them. And then it was over. Each person in attendance was there to support this small girl that had become such a big part of their lives. They hugged her, or patted her head, or kissed her cheek as they left. Destiny never spoke a word and held tightly to Jake's hand the entire time.

Last to leave was Helen. She wanted to make sure she was nearby, just in case Destiny needed her. Helen watched Destiny's face and body language closely. She knew that Destiny would need a lot of time to process what was happening, and had arranged for her to come to therapy more often. Helen hugged Jake and Chrissy good-by and stood in front of Destiny. "You did a nice job reading your poem. I'm so sorry that your mom is gone." Then she hugged Destiny and walked to her car.

The Prestons walked away from the grave to their Suburban. As Destiny opened her door, she turned and waved. Then she climbed in and shut the door.

Destiny's behavior changed. Chrissy would go from the kitchen to the living room and Destiny would follow her. She would go to the bathroom and when she came out, Destiny was sitting by the door waiting for her. She would gather the laundry and run into Destiny if she turned around too fast.

At the Rehab Center, Jake couldn't go anywhere without Destiny right behind him. He often felt her grab onto one of his belt loops as they walked around, checking on birds. She was his shadow. There were even a few times when Jake would stop and Destiny would run into him.

After a while, Jake called a meeting with some of the staff. "You guys have got to help us find ways to keep Destiny occupied. She needs to get back her independence and see that she doesn't need to be an inch from us." Jake ran a hand through his hair. "It's driving me crazy. She even tried to come into the bathroom with me yesterday."

They decided that they would each find ways to involve Destiny so that she would feel needed.

Ruth approached Destiny one morning. "Destiny, I need your help. The birds in the recovery enclosures seem bored. Can you think of any ways that we can challenge them to get their food and exercise their wing muscles?"

Destiny thought for a minute. "Hey, I have an idea. We could make puzzles for them to solve."

"What do you mean?" Ruth asked, scratching her head.

"You know, like make them work for their food, like a game. I saw a video once where zoo workers put a fish in a block of ice for a polar bear. He had to work all day to get that fish out. Like that, only things for birds." Destiny looked serious.

Ruth rubbed her hands together. "I like what I'm hearing. Let's do this!" For the rest of the day, Destiny and Ruth worked together, hiding pieces of meat inside hollow logs, hanging it from perches, tying it to pieces of string and pulling it across their enclosures. Destiny was so focused on the challenge, that she wasn't constantly looking for Chrissy and Jake.

The great horned owl had returned from the university veterinary hospital. Chrissy put him in one of the recovery enclosures. Whenever anyone approached the enclosure, the owl would snap his beak at them and hiss. He would puff up his feathers and stand as tall as he could. While people were close by, he would often open his beak and breathe heavily through his mouth. The feathers on his neck moved in and out at a rapid pace, indicating that he was getting stressed. Destiny wanted to spend time watching him but knew to keep her distance.

The wing had healed completely, but the real work was getting the owl to start using it and build up its strength. He would spread his wings and stretch them, but the right wing didn't match the left one. It dipped down quite a bit. Every time he tried to fly, he fluttered awkwardly to the ground.

Something about the owl drew Destiny to it. She loved the way it was always on alert, always seeing everything that was going on around it. She loved the bright yellow color of its eyes. Its feathers were so soft and even its feet were covered. The tufts of feathers on its head sometimes made Destiny laugh. They looked so much like ears and if it moved just right, you would swear the owl was making fun of you.

One day, when Jake and Destiny went to get the owl out of its cage for physical therapy, they noticed that it was acting differently. "What's wrong with him, Jake?" Destiny asked. "Why isn't he trying to bite us like he usually does?"

The owl just sat there and let Jake pick it up. Jake turned its body. "Look at that," he said. On the owl's chest was a bald patch. "He's pulling his own feathers out. That's strange."

"Is he trying to make a nest?" Destiny asked, looking around the enclosure.

"Most owls take over abandoned nests or use grass and twigs to build nests. This isn't normal behavior for an owl. We need to figure out why he's doing this," Jake said. They carried the bird into the building.

Chrissy was waiting for them. Jake showed her the patch of skin. Chrissy used her fingers to gently probe the area. The owl squirmed and started panting. "I can feel a lump," Chrissy said.

Destiny's brow furrowed. "What are we going to do? Can you give him some medicine?"

"I don't think medicine will make this better, sweetheart," Jake said, rubbing her back. "This is pretty serious." Turning to Chrissy, he said, "What do you think?"

"I agree," Chrissy said. "I think that there is some blockage inside there. He is certainly uncomfortable. We need to act quickly on this, considering his pain level."

"Poor bird," Destiny said. "He can't seem to catch a break. Everything keeps going wrong for him. What are you going to do?"

Jake picked up the phone and put in a call to Dr. Paul at the university. After a brief consultation, Jake hung up. "Dr. Paul agrees with us. This is highly unusual and they want us to bring the owl to them ASAP." He stood up and grabbed his keys.

The next day, Dr. Paul called back. "I'm e-mailing you the x-rays. We had to do surgery to unblock the owl's digestive tract."

Soon, the three of them were gathered around the computer screen on Jake's desk, studying the black and white pictures of the owl's insides. Without its feathers, the owl was actually a very skinny bird. In the pictures, he looked like a Thanksgiving turkey. It would have been funny, except for the big, dark mass that showed up right where his stomach was.

Jake whistled. "I've never seen that before." He enlarged the image and took another look. "Must be painful for him." He rubbed his hand over his chin. He turned to face Destiny. He took her hands in his and looked into her eyes. "Destiny, we have to be prepared for the worst with this. There is a chance that the owl may not live through this. It just happens sometimes, so I want you to know that everyone is trying their best to help him, but it might not be enough."

Destiny's eyes filled with tears. She nodded her head and the tears dripped down her cheeks. She took a deep breath and said, "I know you will try to save her." He held her and closed his eyes.

There was a knock on the office door. Jake opened his eyes and saw Laura standing there. "Hey! It's good to see you, Laura. We just got some bad news about the great horned owl that was injured in the tornado. Destiny could use a distraction to take her mind off of it."

Laura frowned. "I'm so sorry to hear that. Would it be OK if we hang out together for a while, Destiny? Maybe you could give me a tour of the new and improved Rehab Center?"

Destiny nodded. "I guess."

First, she showed Laura the gift shop. Then they went to the warehouse. When she showed Laura how they prepared meals for the birds, Laura looked a little green. Destiny grinned. "You get used to it," she said.

Next, Destiny took Laura through the back door to the flight pens. Laura had lots of questions and Destiny slipped naturally into the role of guide. She shared stories of rescues and gave her updates on where each bird was in their recovery. Laura was impressed with Destiny's knowledge and passion.

They walked to the very back of the property. "This is where the great horned owl got hurt during the tornado. This is a new enclosure, but this is where he was. His wing got broken all over again."

They peeked inside the enclosure. Laura could see several large birds on perches. A tall brown bird turned its head and looked at her with intense yellow eyes. Its long, curved beak made it look almost mean. Destiny saw what Laura was looking at. "That's a golden eagle we brought back from the mountains at the beginning of summer. He was abandoned and left by himself, just like me."

"And just like you, he got to come to this wonderful place to live," Laura said. "Now he's safe and will never be alone again. And neither will you. You are both very lucky to have Jake and Chrissy in your lives."

Destiny actually smiled at this. Then she grew serious again. "Come on, let's go back inside." They made their way back to the building. Destiny opened the door. Jake and Chrissy were standing there.

The look on Chrissy's face stopped Destiny in her tracks. "What's wrong?"

Chrissy knelt in front of her and took Destiny's hands in hers. "The owl didn't make it. He was just too sick. They tried their best, but he's gone, honey. I'm so sorry." Destiny stood like a stone statue. All the color drained from her face. Laura stood behind her and put her hands on Destiny's shoulders. Jake stood next to her with his hands in his pockets. Everyone held their breath, watching Destiny, wondering how she was going to deal with yet another loss.

"How could he do that?" Destiny said. Her voice sounded wooden.

Laura looked confused. "What do you mean?"

"Die like that. How could the owl just leave me like that?"

Jake spoke. "He didn't do it on purpose, honey. He was sick. He didn't want to die. You know how he would hiss and clack his beak at us. He was a fighter. He didn't die because he wanted to. There was a problem in the owl's stomach."

Destiny put her arms around Chrissy's neck and lay her head on Chrissy's shoulder. Chrissy wrapped her arms around Destiny and they rocked back and forth. Not a sound came from Destiny or anyone in the room. The air was heavy with sadness. Sadness for the bird, yes, but more for the little girl who couldn't catch a break.

Finally, Destiny moved back and looked at Jake. "Can we have a funeral for the owl?"

Everyone turned and looked at Laura. She nodded, "I think that would be most appropriate."

"Not here, though," Destiny said.

"What do you mean?" asked Jake.

"We should take him back to his home and set him free like he was meant to be. Can we?"

Chrissy smiled through her tears. "Of course. That's a great idea. I think the owl would like that."

Destiny went to the office and found a sheet of paper in the printer. She sat at Jake's desk and started to write. Laura followed her and looked over her shoulder at the words forming on the page. It was a poem for the owl.

Chapter 39

One morning, at breakfast, Chrissy announced, "Well, it's the first week of August. School will be starting soon. Today we are going shopping for school clothes."

Destiny looked up from her cereal and said, "I don't need new clothes. I can wear what I already have."

"You have been growing like a green bean," Chrissy said. "Your pants will all be high waters by now. You, me, the shopping mall. Let's go."

"Are you coming with us?" Destiny asked Jake.

Jake shook his head, bent over, and held his stomach. "I think I'm coming down with something. It's called Mall Measles. Highly contagious."

Chrissy swatted him with the dishtowel. "You don't have to go. Destiny and I will have fun without you."

Jake stood up and said, "Would you look at that. I'm cured." He grabbed his coffee mug off the counter and walked to the living room.

The trip to the mall was a success. Destiny didn't enjoy it as much as Chrissy did, but she didn't complain. As they were leaving the last store, Chrissy spotted a rack filled with beautiful dresses. She stopped and pulled one down. "What do you think about these?" she asked Destiny.

"I'm NOT wearing that to school," Destiny said, shaking her head vehemently.

"Not for school, silly, for special occasions. Every girl needs a party dress. Let's try one on." After some cajoling, she convinced Destiny to put on a pink dress that had sequins on the skirt.

Chrissy clapped her hands. "Oh, Destiny! That is perfect! You look gorgeous." She pulled Destiny in front of the mirror outside the changing rooms. "What do you think?"

Destiny allowed herself a small smile. The dress was pretty and made her feel special. "It's OK, I guess."

"Sold!" Chrissy said.

With their purchases made, they went home and showed it all to Jake. He oohed and ahhed over all the clothes. When they showed him Destiny's new dress he said, "This is great. I'm glad you got this because I wanted to ask you two out on a date." He winked at Destiny. "Will you go out with me?"

Destiny covered her mouth. She giggled. "Yes."

On Saturday night, Destiny put on the new dress and let Chrissy curl her hair. Chrissy put on a black sheath dress and heels. They walked down the stairs and met Jake at the door. He was wearing a dark suit and white button-down shirt. His tie had tiny owls on it.

"Where are we going?" Destiny asked. "Is it a wedding?" She twirled around the living room.

Chrissy turned and smiled at her. "It's a secret," she said. No matter what Destiny said, or how hard she pleaded, Chrissy and Jake refused to tell her where they were going.

They parked the Suburban in front of a large building with lots of windows. Soft yellow light spilled from inside. A man in a black uniform with a red stripe down the side of the pants opened the door for them. Inside, the floor was covered with large tiles. The tables had white linen cloths on them. There was a stage with an orchestra playing soft music. A dance floor occupied the space in front of the stage. A few couples danced together. The head waiter led them to a table that was right by the stage. Destiny was fascinated by the shiny instruments and swayed to the music. She tried a couple of twirls in her new pink dress. The sequins on the skirt sparkled in the candlelight. She felt like a princess.

She wasn't quite tall enough to sit comfortably at the table, so the waiter brought her a red velvet cushion to sit on. The white china dishes and fancy glasses added a fantasy feel.

"This is like a castle in a Disney movie," Destiny whispered.

"You look like an owl, the way you keep turning to look around you," Jake teased her. There were tall candles on all the tables and over the dance floor was a giant crystal chandelier.

Destiny looked at the table and whispered to Chrissy, "Why are there so many forks?"

Chrissy whispered back, "One for each part of the meal. Start with the one on the outside, and every time they bring you a new plate, use the next one." When the waiter brought her salad, the plate felt like they had just taken it out of the freezer. The next course was prime rib and potatoes. There were tiny carrots in a sweet sauce. For dessert, the waiter set the dish on a stand next to Destiny and pulled out a lighter. Destiny's mouth formed a small 'o' as she watched the dish catch on fire. Soon the flames died out and the waiter served the warm bananas over ice cream. Destiny's eyes were as big as the dessert plate. Jake and Chrissy watched her and delighted in her excitement.

When they could eat no more, the waiters came and cleared the table. They left cups of coffee for the grownups and hot chocolate for Destiny. Destiny couldn't stop smiling. Her stomach was full; her heart was even more full. Then Jake cleared his throat.

"Destiny," he began, "this is a very special place for Chrissy and me. This is where we had our first date, and it's where I proposed to her and she said yes." He paused, picked up Chrissy's hand and kissed it. "We brought you here because we have a very important question to ask you." Destiny frowned. She held her breath. There were butterflies in her stomach. Jake got up from his seat and came over next to Destiny.

He knelt next to her.

"Destiny, we love you with all our hearts. We are better people because you are in our lives. We would like to be your forever family, not just your foster family." He reached into his pocket and pulled out a small heart-shaped box. He opened it. Inside was a small gold ring. The top of the ring was a bird in flight, the wings wrapping around, forming the band of the ring.

"This is a promise ring," he said, his voice becoming raspy. He cleared his throat. Chrissy came to stand behind him, her hand on his shoulder. "We want you to have it as our promise that we will always be there for you, no matter what. We want you to be our daughter. We want to adopt you into our family. What do you think?"

The room had gone quiet. Everything faded away for Destiny. In that moment there was no table, no band, no restaurant. The world consisted only of the three of them. Time stood still. She let it sink in. *These people love me. They want me to be their daughter.* She buried her face in her hands and burst into tears.

She felt herself being lifted and held in strong arms. "Don't cry, sweetheart." She rested her head on Jake's strong shoulders and wrapped her arms around his neck. He could feel her warm breath.

Through her sobs, she managed to say, "I really do want to be your daughter."

Kisses landed on her hair. Jake twirled her around and shouted, "She said yes! I get to be her daddy!" The restaurant erupted in cheers. People around them dabbed tears from their eyes. The orchestra burst into a lively tune. Chrissy came up and hugged Jake and Destiny, making a sandwich of love. They danced together, laughing and crying at the same time.

Jake finally put Destiny down on the floor. He took the ring out of the box and placed it on her finger. "Now it's official," he said. Destiny looked down at the ring. She noticed that it was an owl. Each tiny feather was etched in the metal and his tiny head was perfect. It wasn't a great horned owl; she could tell because it didn't have feather tufts on its head. She hugged both Jake and Chrissy saying, "Thank you!" over and over again.

Their waiter returned to the table with a bottle of champagne and beautiful crystal glasses for the adults. He carried a similar glass filled with sparkling grape juice for Destiny. "The manager says it's on the house. Congratulations." Many of the people in the restaurant came over to the table to congratulate them as well.

Destiny fell asleep on the car ride home. Jake carried her up to her room. He laid her on the bed and Chrissy gently took off her shoes. They pulled the purple comforter over her. They kissed her forehead softly and tiptoed out of the room, closing the door gently behind them.

Jake pulled Chrissy into his arms as they stood in the hall outside Destiny's bedroom. "We have a daughter," Chrissy said. She kissed Jake. He kissed her back.

"This feels so right," he said. They held each other for a long time.

On Monday morning, they had an appointment with the judge. When they arrived at the courthouse, there was a small crowd of people waiting for them. As they came closer, Destiny recognized Miss Laura and Helen and Ruth and Sharon from the Rehab Center. The rest of the people were strangers to her. She took Chrissy's hand and held it tight.

"Destiny, meet your grandparents," Chrissy said. She introduced her parents and Jake's parents as well as some of their brothers and sisters. Each one shook Destiny's hand. The last person to be introduced was Mr. Carter, their lawyer. He led the way to the courtroom.

Destiny felt small in the giant room. There were rows of long wooden benches and tall windows were streaming in sunlight. The judge's bench was very tall and intimidating looking. Everyone found seats on the benches and waited for the judge. Soon a kindly looking man with white hair and glasses came in through a hidden door. He was wearing a black robe over his clothes. Everyone stood up to show their respect.

The judge sat down and motioned for them to do the same. "I'm Judge Mallory. I understand there's a family here that is getting a little bigger today. Please come forward."

Jake, Chrissy, and Destiny stepped through a little swinging gate that separated the seating area from the front of the courtroom. The stood in a line with their lawyer. Mr. Carter introduced the family to Judge Mallory. Then he asked each of them to tell the judge a little about themselves.

"I'm Jacob Preston. My wife, Chrissy, and I run the Raptor Rehabilitation Center here in town. We met Destiny close to a year ago. We had just received our clearance to become foster parents. Destiny is our first foster child. We fell in love with her and after her mother passed away this summer, we decided that we wanted – no – needed her to be a permanent part of our family." Jake ducked his head down, cleared his throat, and wiped a tear from his face.

Chrissy spoke up. "I'm Christina Preston, Your Honor. Jake and I are Licensed Wildlife Rehabilitators. Destiny came to us through our friend, Laura Saunders, who happened to be Destiny's caseworker through the Child Protective Services office. The timing was perfect and we became Destiny's foster parents the same night we met her. Now we just want to make official what we already feel, that she is our daughter." Chrissy wrapped her arm around Destiny's shoulder and held her tight to her side.

The judge listened carefully. He smiled at the little family standing in front of him. "Destiny, please come here," he said, motioning with his hand.

Destiny looked at Jake and Chrissy. They nodded their heads and pointed to the stairs leading up to the judge's bench. She walked slowly up the steps, her shoes making loud sounds on the wooden floor, and stood in front of the judge. Her eyes were large and scared. Judge

Mallory put his arm around Destiny and drew her to his side. They looked out over the courtroom. "Look at all these people, Destiny. They love you very much and want you to be a part of their family. Is that what you want?"

Destiny nodded her head. "Yes, sir, I do," she said in a small voice. "I want to be their little girl."

"Then let's make that happen," the judge said. Turning his attention to Jake and Chrissy, he said, "You understand that you will be this lovely child's permanent family? That you will care for her physical, emotional, spiritual, and mental needs for the rest of her childhood? Even if your marriage doesn't make it, both of you will be forever this little girl's parents and will treat her as such?"

Jake and Chrissy held hands. They nodded their heads vigorously. "We do, Your Honor! It will be our pleasure to take care of Destiny. She is our daughter!" Jake said.

The judge handed Destiny a large wooden gavel and showed her how to bang it on a circle of wood on his desk. He said, "I declare that the adoption of Destiny Preston, by Jacob and Christina Preston to be final!" Destiny banged the gavel three times. Everyone cheered and clapped their hands. Judge Mallory hugged Destiny, then led her down the stairs to her new parents. They all stood in front of the judge's bench for pictures.

Destiny was seeing stars from all the camera flashes. She was hugged and kissed too many times to count. She was beginning to feel anxious from all the attention. She was relieved when they left the courtroom to sign some papers in the judge's chambers.

As they were finishing up, Jake's phone rang. He pulled it out of his pocket to see who it was. It was the Rehab Center. "Hey," he said. "Can I call you back? We're with the judge." The person on the other end kept talking. Jake listened for a few seconds, then his face grew serious. "Ok, we'll be there in fifteen minutes."

Chrissy looked at him quizzically. "There's some sort of emergency out at the Rehab Center. Jeremy sounded frantic and they need us to come ASAP."

"They can't handle it by themselves? Today of all days?" Chrissy asked, putting her hands on her hips.

Jake shook his head. "Didn't sound like it."

"Let's go," Chrissy sighed.

They quickly hugged their family and friends and rushed to the car. "Did Jeremy say what the emergency was?" Chrissy asked.

Jake shook his head, concentrating on moving through traffic. They stopped at a red light. Turning to Chrissy, he said, "No, he just said they had a situation that they couldn't deal with and they needed us right away. He made it sound really bad." The light turned green and the car surged ahead.

They turned the final corner and headed towards the blue metal building. They could see that the garage door on the front was open. As they got closer, they saw people milling around inside. "What the heck?" Jake said, putting the Suburban in park.

They walked to the building and the crowd inside started clapping and yelled, "Congratulations!" There were pink streamers strung throughout the space. Large tables had been set up and a big cake sat on a table covered with a pink cloth. Music started to play in the background and the whole staff came forward and tried to hug the family at once. It was happy chaos for a while. Jake and Chrissy's families came in and so did Helen and Laura. They had been in on the surprise the whole time.

Jeremy looked sheepish when he finally got his turn to hug Jake and Chrissy. "Sorry about the bogus call, Boss. It was the only way we could figure out to get you to come over here today. Since we couldn't all be at the courthouse, this seemed to be the right thing to do."

Jake and Chrissy wandered over to the cake table. The cake was a large rectangle edged in pink. It said 'IT'S A GIRL!' on the top. Instead of a pair of baby booties like you see at baby showers, someone had taken a picture of Destiny and turned it into an edible photo. The picture showed Destiny next to a cage with the great horned owl. It was a rare photo where Destiny was smiling. She had her head thrown back, eyes closed and laughing. The owl had a particularly perturbed look on its face.

Destiny was a little timid with the number of people around her. She'd never had this much attention given to her before, but these were people she knew, her friends and now her new family. She ate three pieces of cake and soon there was icing in her hair. She didn't care in the least.

When speakers started blaring her favorite song, she ran over to Jake and got him to dance with her. Chrissy joined them, then Jeremy grabbed someone. Soon everyone was jumping around, singing along.

The afternoon flew by. Everyone laughed and hugged and told stories about Jake, Chrissy, and Destiny. As the party wound down, Jake held Destiny close and whispered in her ear, "I love you."

Destiny closed her eyes and let the words wash over her.

Chapter 40

"Destiny Preston?" the teacher called. She was taking roll. Destiny smiled and raised her hand. Her classmates, many of whom had been in her class the year before, looked around for the new girl. When they saw Destiny raising her hand, their mouths opened in shock. They hardly recognized this smiling, clean girl in the new, yellow sundress.

There were butterflies in her stomach as she settled into her seat. She felt like a whole new person. She had a home with parents who loved her; she felt safe for the first time in her life. There was no question that when she went home, she would have food to eat and a warm place to sleep.

After school, she met with Helen to discuss her new class. There was so much to talk about.

"How was the first day back to school?" Helen asked. She was sitting on the couch with her legs crossed. Destiny sat in the armchair across from her.

Destiny giggled. "You should have seen the look on the kids' faces when the teacher called my new name. Their mouths were open! It's hard to believe that's me!"

Helen laughed. "I'll bet they thought they had a new student."

Destiny nodded. "It was like I was playing a practical joke on them or something. A couple of girls wanted me to sit with them at lunch. They asked me what happened. I told them I was adopted!" There was a look of pride on her face.

"Did the rest of the day go well?" Helen wanted to know.

"Yeah, first days are always easy. Teachers hand out books and go over rules and stuff. Nothing big, really. We got to draw pictures of ourselves as students. I liked that," Destiny said. She played with the ends of the ribbon around her waist. "I wish every day could be this way."

"You know it won't be. There will be days when you don't understand, or get something wrong. We should come up with a plan for how to handle that," Helen said. They spent the rest of the session rehearsing strategies for Destiny to use on those tough days.

As their time was winding down, Destiny said, "I have something for you." She hopped off her chair and went over to the door, where she had dropped her backpack. She opened it and came back holding the stuffed cat. Shyly, she held it out to Helen. "I'm sorry I took this from you. You can have it back now. I have a new cat, a real one."

Helen took the stuffed animal from her and set it on her lap. She patted the couch next to her and said, "Sit by me. I'd love to hear the story of the real Fur Ball."

Destiny sat next to her and pulled her knees up to her chest. She looked at the toy and thought for a minute.

"When I was littler, like 6 or something, things started to get bad for me and my mom, you know? She lost her job. We couldn't stay there because of the rent money. So, we were staying in our car. Then some people came and hooked the car onto a big truck and took it away. Mom screamed at the guy, but he took it anyway. Mom started hanging out with creepy guys and we ended up living in that yucky house." Destiny shifted herself around to sit on her knees, facing Helen.

"She started getting mad all the time. Yelling at me. Telling me it was my fault. She said she wished I'd never been born. She stopped paying attention to me most of the time. When she did, she told me that I ruined her life and I caused all these bad things to happen. She would scream at me if I told her I was hungry or cold. One night she actually threw me out of the house and locked the door. I cried and banged on the door, but she wouldn't let me in."

"That must have been hard for you," Helen said, softly. She reached for a tissue on the coffee table.

Destiny shrugged. "I guess. There was an old shed in the backyard. When she wouldn't let me in, I went in the shed to find somewhere to sleep. I found an old blanket. I sat there in the dark, scared. Then I heard this tiny little meow. I felt something bump against my hand. There was this orange cat looking at me. It climbed under the blanket with me and curled up. It purred and talked to me all night."

Helen pictured a cold, scared, little girl sitting in that shed. She put her hand on the toy cat in her lap and said a silent thank you to the furry little angel that had found her that night.

Destiny continued. "Ever since that night, Fur Ball would hang around and keep me company. I would bring him treats from school. He was my only friend. He wasn't a picky eater. His favorite was cheese, though. You know those orange sticks they give you for breakfast?" Helen nodded, not trusting her voice.

"That day when I was in here, the day you told me my mom died? I saw this toy sticking out of the toy box, just like Fur Ball peeking out of the shed. I imagined it was him. I'm sorry I took it." She looked up at Helen.

Helen wrapped her arms around Destiny and held her tight. "Don't apologize. I'm so glad you found a friend to help you through that tough time. We'll put Fur Ball the Second in a special place in here so he can watch over us." She stood up and cleared a space on her bookshelf. She placed the cat on the shelf and adjusted it so that it looked like a real cat sleeping there.

Chapter 41

One Saturday in October, Chrissy told Destiny, "It's time for Owl-o-ween!"

Destiny looked up from her cereal bowl. "What's that?"

Chrissy sat down at the table and said, "It's when we have an open house at the Rehab Center and invite the public in to see some of the birds and trick-or-treat in their costumes. We have it the Saturday before Halloween. What do you think? Sounds fun, right?"

"Do I get to wear a costume?" Destiny asked.

"Yup. We all do. We hand out candy, too. Let's go get Jake and shop for costumes today," Chrissy said.

"Aren't you too old for costumes?" Destiny asked, following her up the stairs.

Chrissy shook her head. "You are never too old to have fun!"

Jake, Chrissy, and Destiny drove to the party store. They found racks and racks of costumes. Destiny was a little overwhelmed. They wandered around the store for a while, just looking.

"Want to be a pirate?" Jake asked, holding up a black and white striped vest and an eye patch. Destiny shook her head.

Chrissy said, "Ooh, what about a mermaid. This one has a wig!" Destiny rejected that one, too.

"I know what I want to be," Chrissy said. She held up a long, red velvet dress with a mask that looked like a bird beak. "Birdwoman!"

Jake pulled a costume down that had a black vest with tattoo sleeves and a blond mullet wig. "I think this is perfect for me. I'm the biker type, right?" He pretended to rev a bike and made Chrissy and Destiny laugh.

"What about you, Destiny? See anything you like?" Chrissy asked.

Destiny timidly touched a costume. "Maybe this one?" It was a superhero cape and mask.

Jake smiled. "Perfect. You are my superhero."

The Saturday of the open house was beautiful. There wasn't a cloud in the sky, and the forecast said that the temperatures would be warmer than normal for October. The volunteers and staff at the Rehab Center all arrived early to move crates and equipment to set up for the open house. Jeremy handed Destiny a package of Halloween decorations and a roll of tape. "Go hang these all over the place," he said. Soon there were ghosts and bats and spiders hanging from every surface.

Destiny went into the office to change into her costume. She was still shy around people she didn't know and was glad that her mask would hide her face. She filled her bucket with candy. There were butterflies in her stomach as she thought about all the people that were coming to see the birds. Her birds. A smile played across her face. She remembered the first time she had come here and how amazed she had been.

She went out into the warehouse and found her station, right next to the tiny little red Eastern screech owl. Soon her bucket of candy was empty. She went back to the office to get some more. Coming out, she carefully closed the door. As she turned around, she almost ran into someone dressed as a ghost. "Happy Halloween," the ghost said, waving its arms and trying to sound spooky.

Destiny wrapped her arms around the ghost and squeezed. "Happy Halloween, Miss Laura," she said.

The ghost's shoulders slumped. "Darn, I thought I could scare you." Laura pulled off the sheet and smiled at Destiny. "You look very cute as a superhero."

"Thank you," Destiny said. "Watch this!" She spread her arms out as wide as the hallway would let her and spun around. "Did you see my cape? It's hooked to my wrists. It really looks like I'm flying, especially when I run."

Laura admired the costume from all angles and agreed that it really did look like she was flying. In her mind, she was thinking about how different this Destiny was from the one she had met in the principal's office wearing a grungy green hoodie with a sullen look on her face. She was almost unrecognizable as that girl now.

The hallway was getting crowded as people were trying to make their way to the gift shop. Destiny and Laura walked to the warehouse. "It's been a long time since I've been here. Want to show me what's new?" Laura asked.

Destiny slipped her hand into Laura's and smiled up at her. "I don't want you to get lost in the crowd," she said.

Their first stop was the old barn owl. "This is Grandpa, Miss Laura. He is a great foster parent. He never gets mad or anything, but he teaches the owlets how to hunt and stuff. He makes the cutest noises when he tucks them under his wings. He's very protective of them, but he doesn't let them mess around or anything." Destiny giggled and said, "Too bad he can't work for you!" Laura laughed.

Then she tugged on Laura's hand again and took her to see the small Eastern screech owl. "I call this one Tiny. When we go out to libraries and stuff, Chrissy and Jake let me tell everyone about him," she said. Then she whispered, "I know we aren't supposed to give them names, but I can't help it."

Chrissy spotted them in the crowd and came swishing over in her red dress. She took off her mask and hugged Laura and Destiny. "Having fun?" she asked. "This crowd is great! We always have such a big turnout for this event. I love seeing all the kids in their costumes."

A happy squeal made them turn around. A little girl in a frilly pink princess costume, complete with crown and scepter, came running towards them. "Destiny! We came to see you!" It was Julie, with Derrick, dressed as a vampire, Grandpa Ben, and Grandma Lucy. The two girls hugged and jumped around excitely.

Grandpa Ben said, "This is quite the place!"

Destiny nodded and said, "Let me show you!" She took off and everyone followed her. She became the tour guide for the group.

While they wandered around and listened to Destiny, Laura asked Grandma Lucy, "How is Susan doing?"

"She's hanging in there. The treatments are making her very weak. She barely has enough energy to walk around the house. She really wanted to come today, too. She would be so proud of how well Destiny is doing." Grandma Lucy smiled at the two girls, who were studying a display of tail feathers. She called out, "Girls, look at me!" She snapped a picture with her phone.

Chrissy nodded. "We are all proud of her. She is making such great progress. We still see signs from her past every once in a while, but she is handling the bumps in the road so much better."

Jeremy came over to ask Chrissy a question. "Excuse, me," she said and followed Jeremy to another part of the room.

"Come see the birds' egg display I helped with," Destiny said, pulling Julie along after her. The group went over to another table that had been draped with black cloth. There were baskets set out on the table with eggs from different birds. Each basket had a little card telling what kind of bird laid the egg, ranging from owls all the way up to a giant ostrich egg. All of them were white, except for the emu egg, which was a dark grayish color. Destiny pointed to the hand-lettered signs. "I made those," she said, proudly.

Laura stood in the back of the group, watching Destiny. She saw how she interacted with her friends, the staff, and volunteers. She saw a little girl who was finally where she needed to be, where she was meant to be. These people loved her and valued her.

Jake saw them and came over. Destiny flung her arms around his middle and hugged him tightly. They both had huge grins on their faces. He reached around Destiny and hugged Laura. "Thanks for coming, Laura. Isn't this great?" He looked around the warehouse.

Laura agreed, "This is the best thing I've seen in a long time." But she wasn't looking at the crowd, the displays, or the birds. She was looking at Jake and Destiny. "This makes my heart so happy." Tears welled up in her eyes. She looked at her watch. "I hate to leave so soon, but I have to go to a meeting. Thanks for inviting me."

"Let's walk her to her car," Jake said to Destiny. They went through the open garage door to the parking lot. She hugged Jake and Destiny again and got in her car. As she was leaving, she watched Destiny running down the sidewalk, back to the party. Her arms were outstretched and her cape was flapping behind her. Laura smiled. "You are finally free, little one. Free as a bird."

About the Author

Missy Tarantino is a full-time teacher in Northern Colorado. She works with children from all over the world, helping them learn English. When she isn't in the classroom, you can find her on the race course, driving one of her husband's hand-built race cars.

You can connect with me on:

🌐 https://missytarantino.com

f http://facebook.com/MissyWritesBooks

Subscribe to my newsletter:

✉ https://landing.mailerlite.com/webforms/landing/n4cot4

Also by Missy Tarantino

Missy writes for both children and adults. Her Traveling Trunk series introduces children to cultures all around the world. For the grown-ups, she writes both mysteries and young adult fiction.

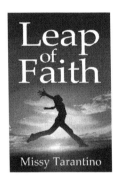

Leap of Faith

A broken car, a broken relationship. Is there glue for these things?

Mary Beth just wants to hide under the covers until things get better. Over breakfast in their favorite café, Mary Beth's best friend hatches a plan to help get her life back together. When her family, mostly her sister, expresses their doubts about her making something of herself, Mary Beth decides to take the plunge.

Quitting her job is her first step towards taking control of her life. But, a stubborn new client causes her to second guess her decisions.

Will Mary Beth regret her decision to leave all that is familiar and set a new path for her life?

Family Collateral

Alfie has a secret. Will she use it to save her family or do what is right?

On a visit to the museum, Alfie discovers a cold case that pulls at her heartstrings when she sees the photo of a 7-year-old who was killed almost 100 years ago. But when her mother discovers that she is straying from her path of becoming a lawyer, she forbids Alfie from working on the case.

Alfie is torn between doing what is right and doing what is easy. She tries to please her mother but finds it impossible to forget the face in the photograph. Then she discovers a secret that could destroy her family. Will she burn the evidence or face her mother's fury?

Made in the USA
Middletown, DE
25 April 2022

64728393R00132